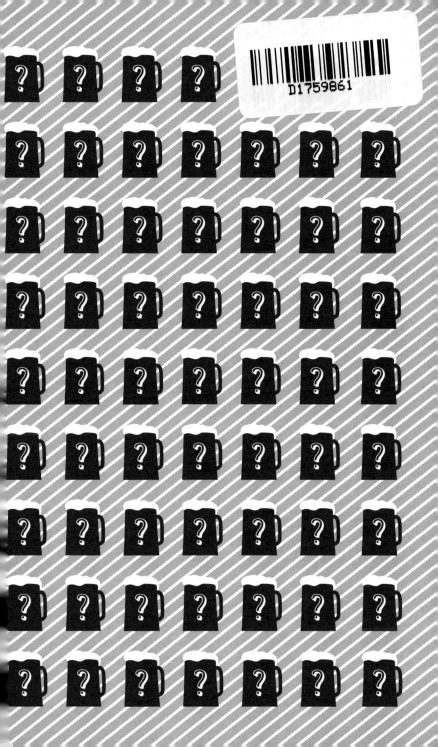

LES ? PALMER

HOW TO
WIN YOUR
PUB QUIZ

PORTICO

First published in the United Kingdom in 2013 by
Portico Books
10 Southcombe Street
London
W14 0RA

An imprint of Anova Books Company Ltd

ISBN 9781907554933

A CIP catalogue record for this book is available from the British Library.

10 9 8 7 6 5 4 3 2 1

Printed and bound by 1010 Printing International Ltd, China

This book can be ordered direct from the publisher at
www.anovabooks.com

CONTENTS

HELLO THERE, QUIZZERS!

Pub quizzes are on the up and have been for many years. Once so rare, they are now ubiquitous to the point where there are really only three types of pub – boarded-up pubs, gastro pubs and pubs that do quizzes. During these austere times those 'Quiz Night Monday' signs on pub forecourts are like beacons of hope, pointing the way to welcoming havens where ordinary, decent folk can enjoy a life-affirming experience. After all, what better way to banish those recessionary woes than to earn your team critical points on the Joker Round by successfully remembering that the vacuum cleaner in *Teletubbies* is called Noo-Noo, with the vague hope that you might win a free meal for two (drinks not included) at the end of the evening?

The book you are holding in your hand (probably while on the loo) is a unique celebration of the British pub quiz and its burgeoning army of aficionados. But it is more than that, because it is also rooted in the premise that the very best type of pub quiz is one that *your* team ends up winning. This book provides a step-by-step guide to increasing both your personal quizzing prowess and that of your team until you become the smug gits who all the other teams desperately want to knock off their perch. You will become the ultimate champions – and people will hate you for it! This book describes a range of hints, tips and techniques that will help convert you from a pub quiz also-ran into a rapacious fact-crunching monster. Moreover, it will examine how your team can improve collectively to become a wholly integrated and finely honed pub-quiz-winning machine.

But what, you might ask, are my credentials for writing such a book? Well, let me start with a confession. My name is Les and I am a quizaholic. I simply love doing pub quizzes. As soon as one has finished I'm counting the days, or more usually the hours, until the next one is due to start. Inevitably, I find that the long periods between quiz nights weigh heavy. Sure, I can kill time doing my quiz fact drills – after all, I wouldn't want to slip up on something obvious like Best Film Oscar 1934 (*It Happened One Night*, which of course won all four main awards that year, plus Best Screenplay) or World Darts Champion 2003 (a surprise victory for Canadian outsider John 'Darth Maple' Part). But, fun though that is, it cannot compete with the adrenalin-soaked thrill of the quiz itself.

Now, I believe I am sufficiently self-aware to recognise that by making such an admission I run the risk of being perceived as a fact-obsessed Billy No-Mates (though when I raised this concern with my wide circle of friends, he assured me that this was not the case). But, either way, pub quizzing is what I do, or as Americans like to say: 'It's my jahhhb'. (It's really not my job – it's just that I behave like it is sometimes. Well, most of the time actually.)

But the great thing about pub quizzing is that it's a broad church and loads of perfectly normal and well-balanced people do it as well! According to a recent survey[1], 42 per cent of pubs host a weekly quiz, so pub quizzing is not the sole preserve of some rarefied Bullingdon Club-style elite. Rather, anyone can do it, and lots of people do, enjoying many a wonderful evening in the process.

My own Damascene conversion came about 15 years ago. Until then, I'd never really 'got' pub quizzes, even though I'd been forced to sit through the odd one or two. I used to think they were the preserve of pimply inadequates who needed to get out more, or preferably less. In fact, I would find the whole ritual weird and rather futile, and some of the people a bit scary. But one night I was invited to join a pub quiz team by a friend I owed a favour to, so my usual 'I'm busy defrosting my freezer that night' excuse wouldn't cut it. I duly trooped along with zero expectations, only to find myself hooked by about the fifth question of the first round (Pot Luck, I recall – I think the question was: 'Which type of timepiece has the most moving parts?' Answer: An hourglass).

The strange thing is that I wasn't very good – in fact I was virtually useless. Now, whenever I try something new, failure is normally sufficient to send me scuttling off with my tail between my legs, vowing never to return – 'If at first you don't succeed, give up'. But that night something clicked. For a start, I found the questions truly fascinating, even though I knew so few of the answers. And, to my amazement, I genuinely enjoyed the company and the banter. Specifically, I remember savouring the prospect of my second pint of Ruttocks Old Obnoxious as I experienced a moment of pure euphoria. I simply allowed my gaze to drift around the room, settling languidly on some of my fellow quizzers with their comb-overs and interesting facial hair. Then I looked at the men, and I thought: 'I've come home.'

These warm feelings duly sustained me for a number of blissfully happy years. And then, gradually, a creeping dissatisfaction began to gnaw away at my gut because, although my team continued to enjoy our pub quizzing, something was missing – and that something was the scent of victory! Every week, we would put in a perfectly decent performance only to finish in mid-table, well off the podium prizes but way too high for the consolation sweets. Eventually, something had to change, so I started to take a keen interest in the types of team that contested the top spot every week – I'm talking here about the most fanatical type of quizzer for whom forgetting that it was Percy Shaw who invented the cat's eye while Sir Isaac Newton designed the cat flap represents failure of the most abject kind (cat-astrophic, even). And I thought: 'I want to be like you.'

So, over a period of several years, I subjected myself to an intensive programme of self-improvement, which eventually bore fruit, albeit at the expense of a small part of my sanity, my family life and my career. But the upshot was that, over time, I too became a crusty middle-aged pub-quiz-winning git. Now the time has come to share my experience with you in the form of this self-help manual to fulfilling your quizzing potential. So whether you are just looking for a small increase in your team's performance level, or you want to go the whole nine yards and become the type of serial pub quiz winners that other teams love to hate, there will be something in this book for you.

Happy quizzing. But, more importantly ...

Go and ruddy well win!

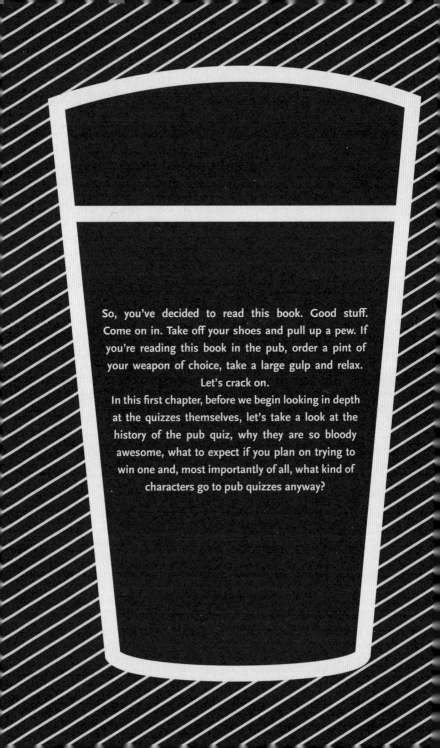

So, you've decided to read this book. Good stuff.
Come on in. Take off your shoes and pull up a pew. If
you're reading this book in the pub, order a pint of
your weapon of choice, take a large gulp and relax.
Let's crack on.

In this first chapter, before we begin looking in depth
at the quizzes themselves, let's take a look at the
history of the pub quiz, why they are so bloody
awesome, what to expect if you plan on trying to
win one and, most importantly of all, what kind of
characters go to pub quizzes anyway?

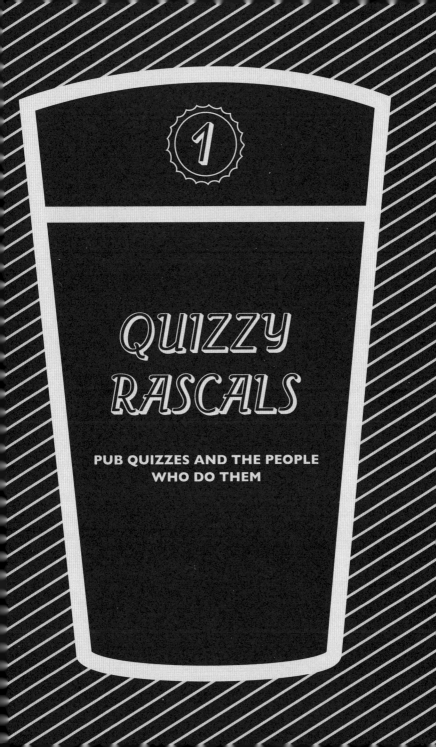

1

QUIZZY RASCALS

PUB QUIZZES AND THE PEOPLE WHO DO THEM

IMAGINE you are in a strange town, maybe on business or enjoying a holiday with your family. It's 8pm-ish and you decide to pop into a local pub that's caught your eye to quietly while away an hour or two. Whether your day has been fulfilling or stressful, what could be better than an alcoholic beverage to round things off and unwind a little?

You step inside, and the pub's external promise is immediately fulfilled. It's an attractive, inviting place with a wide range of beers, a decent selection of wines and an appealing menu. An open fire is roaring away, the lighting is nicely subdued and the background music is pleasant and unobtrusive. And you've managed to bag a really nice table close to the fire. Feeling at one with the world, you settle in, take a sip of your beer and hunker down for a relaxing evening.

After a few minutes, though, you start to detect a change. Several groups of people are coming into the pub – two fifty-something couples, a group of youngsters, a few elderly folk, and then some middle-aged blokes – whole gangs of them, in fact. You also notice that the lighting has suddenly become much brighter and the music has stopped. Slowly, the penny starts to drop and you feel a shudder of apprehension. Sure enough, your worst fears are confirmed as, at 8.20 on the dot, a bumptious-looking individual sets up at the table next to you with a microphone and utters the dreaded words: *'One two, one two. Tonight's quiz will start in ten minutes.'*

Your chin hits the table and your body crumples in on itself. 'Argh! No! Not again! Why does this keep happening to me? What is it with these bloody people and their flippin' quizzes? Why can't they just be normal and go for a drink like anyone else? Or stay at home and watch *Mastermind*, rather than inflict their obsession on the rest of us? Soon, they'll be shouting the odds about some question they didn't like, or bickering over the marking, or whingeing about people Googling the answers on their smartphones. Then they'll start arguing among themselves, saying things like: "I *told* you it was Bert Lahr who played the Cowardly Lion, but would you listen ..." And for the next two hours I'll have to put up with that nit next to me bellowing into his mic and covering me in phlegm. Why do they have to do it? And why must they take it all so seriously? Can't they get a sodding life and leave me to enjoy my pint in peace?'

Ah yes, the pub quizzer – what a piece of work! How is it that he's able to name all eight of Santa's original reindeer (i.e. excluding Rudolph) without pausing for breath, or to reel off every Commonwealth Games' venue in order since they started in 1930 (they were, of course, held in Hamilton, Ontario, that year). And why does he get so swept up in the whole thing, eyes bulging as he tries to dredge the capital of Burkina Faso out from his innermost depths (Ouagadougou, since you ask, which, coincidentally, happens to be the sound emitted during the dredging process).

Whatever you think about them, pub quizzes are here to stay and, as the old adage goes: 'If you can't beat 'em, join 'em', so if you're a pub quiz agnostic I hope this book encourages you to give them a try, because it really can be tremendous fun. But perhaps the expression: 'If you've already joined 'em, why not beat 'em!' best sums up what this book is about, namely to help existing quizzers improve their team's performance so they can stick it to those irritating bastards in the corner who win every week.

A Brief History of the Pub Quiz

So, how has the pub quiz evolved into the phenomenon that it has now become? Following extensive research involving an in-depth trawl through numerous archives, coupled with a minutely forensic examination of a wide range of original manuscripts (supplemented by 30 minutes on Wikipedia), I have managed to piece together the following sequence of historic pub quiz milestones:

- **9th century:** Alfred the Great, as part of his quest to bring culture and literacy to England, attempts to introduce the pub quiz into Wessex, but the inaugural evening is ruined by an unfortunate cake-burning incident, which prevents refreshments being served at the break.

- **1066, Hastings:** England is conquered by a man called Norman, who establishes a dynasty of winning pub quiz team captains that survives to this day.

- **15th-century Southern Europe:** earliest recorded 'true or false' question, namely: 'The Earth is flat – true or false?'. Two points to be awarded for the correct answer (true). An incorrect answer is worth no points, though players will receive a consolation visit from the Spanish Inquisition.

- **Early 16th-century Northern Europe:** evidence of the first tie-break question has recently come to light in the form of a manuscript which reads: 'Question: How many theses did Martin Luther nail to the door of the church at Wittenburg? Answer: 95 (if used during the main part of the quiz, teams may be allowed up to five theses either side)'.

- **Mid-16th-century England:** the first handout round is introduced, entitled 'Identify the Traitor or Heretic', whereby real heads or charred body parts are passed around the teams for identification.

- **Early 17th-century Stratford-on-Avon:** William Shakespeare's team is so successful that his local pub (Ye Olde Stratford Olympick Hamlet) refuses to serve him, resulting in one of the earliest recorded *Sun* headlines – You're Bard!

- **Early 19th-century:** pub quiz mania sweeps the UK, as evidenced by Nelson's dying words: 'Quiz me, Hardy.'

OK, I am prepared to concede that one or two of these facts might be somewhat apocryphal, but by the time we reach the 20th century we are back on firmer ground.

BUT SERIOUSLY...

Pub quizzes started to sporadically appear from around the middle of the 20th century, and by the 1980s were becoming established as a staple element of pub entertainment. But it's during the last 20 years or so that they have really taken off. It is estimated that over 20,000 pub quizzes are held each week[2], which, assuming an average ten teams per quiz and four players per team, would equate to a tally of about 800,000 regular pub quizzers.

Beyond that, millions more tune into popular TV quiz shows like *Eggheads*, *The Chase* and *Who Wants to Be a Millionaire?* This has given rise to new levels of that time-honoured pastime of 'Shouting at the Telly' which sometimes even exceed those associated with football ('NO, YOU TWAT – KARL WAS NOT THE OLDEST OF THE MARX BROTHERS!'). And what about quiz books? These days every bookshop seems to stock shelf-loads of them, with new ones coming out all the time. It is really quite remarkable that so many unique titles can be achieved by juggling the words 'best', 'ultimate', 'pub', 'family', 'quiz', 'trivia', 'book' and 'ever'.

So, why are pub quizzes now so widespread across the UK? You only have to read the local newspaper to know that thousands of pubs have closed during the last few years alone in the wake of cheap supermarket booze, fewer people being prepared to drink and drive, the rise of technology-driven home entertainment, the smoking ban and, of course, the recession, while some of the best-run establishments are merely treading water. Under such pressures publicans have had to put greater effort into devising creative forms of entertainment in order to attract the punters back into their establishments ... and this is where quizzes come in.

GREAT THINGS ABOUT PUB QUIZZES

1. Spending the evening with well-rounded, intelligent people
Plus several socially awkward geeks, obviously. It is commonly accepted that most pub quizzers, particularly the successful ones, are more comfortable dealing with facts than people. For them the great thing about quiz night is that they don't have to bother with small talk because they are entirely focused on the quiz, and when they are required to converse they can do so with people of a similar ilk, so it's a win-win situation.

2. Comical team names
One of the great things about pub quizzers is their ingenuity in devising new and funny names for their teams, some of which are printable. By way of a taster, one of my current favourites is 'Quiztopher BigWins', but there are literally tens of other funny ones and a selection of the best/worst (delete as applicable) of these can be found further on in the book.

3. Team Spirit

It is a truly heart-warming experience to witness the evolution of a pub quiz team, as a bunch of shoe-gazing oddballs steadily morphs into a vibrant, wholly engaged and fully integrated unit. Strong team dynamics can be the key to finding that extra 1 per cent of improvement needed to become pub quiz winners, and this too will be discussed in a later chapter. But, basically, you need a team full of unique *University Challenge* nerds who also like to watch sport, telly and drink beer.

4. Discovering fascinating facts

Not a lot of people know stuff like this:

🍺 Al Capone was a second-hand furniture salesman, at least according to his business card

🍺 The maiden name of Buzz Aldrin's mother was Moon

🍺 Hitler was *Time Magazine*'s 'Man of the Year' in 1938.

People who consider themselves reasonably intelligent may find their first exposure to a pub quiz to be a horribly chastening experience. They may be capable of delivering an informed analysis of the root of the Eurozone crisis and outlining the pros and cons of a range of fiscal or structural alternatives, but those things are unlikely to come up, especially if you're in Doncaster. If they don't know that SuperTed's mortal enemy was Texas Pete, they won't have a prayer. But if that's you, do not despair! Come the end of this book you'll be able to fillet out this type of quiz-winning trivia from the mass of useless crapformation that is out there. Well, that's the plan.

5. Improving your knowledge

There are a variety of mental Derren Brown-esque techniques, cheats and tricks for learning and retaining new facts so that your team can benefit from a massive improvement in your quizzing prowess. Stuff like eidetic memory recall, mind-mapping, self-hypnosis, lateral thinking, randomising, NLP and kinaesthetics will help you become a more creative and intelligent thinker. But to be quite frank, we are only trying to get you to win a pub quiz, not become a doctor, so instead of trying to learn lots of complicated tricky stuff you'll just end up forgetting, I'll give you loads of cool mnemonics that will help you out of many a sticky anomia-based situation (that means when its stuck on the tip of your tongue – see, you're learning already). These methods, which range from the stunningly simple to the totally tragic, are described fully in later chapters.

6. Super-Annoyingly Difficult Questions

Coming up with decent questions can be a ball-ache, but quizmasters should try to remember that each question is an opportunity to dazzle. The best challenging questions are the ones you think you know, or thought you knew, but now can't quite remember, and provoke the response, 'Ah, I know this! Be quiet … It'll come to me!' Indeed, just one genuinely thought-provoking question can leave players with a terrific memory to take away from their night's quizzing. How about: 'Which Shakespeare character can be found between a Canadian city and a 1980s car?' (the answer is tucked away in one of the later chapters, so I'm afraid you'll just have to read on!). How's that for annoying?

7. Entertaining Rounds

There is nothing wrong with standard rounds such as History, Geography, Sport or Movies, but a well-constructed and more novel round can provide a refreshing change. Take the following 'Connections' round, for example:

1. Which people are known as Inuit in their own language? Answer = Eskimo

2. What is the name of the largest peninsula in Mexico? Answer = Yucatan

3. Which new nation emerged in 2011 with the capital Juba? Answer = South Sudan

4. Which 80s band was fronted by David Sylvian? Answer = Japan

5. What connects the above answers? Answer = 'Hit Me with Your Rhythm Stick' (by Ian Dury and the Blockheads)

8. Terrific Banter

Pub quizzers have something of a reputation for being a motley collection of nerds and pointyheads for whom the sense-of-humour bypass is the busiest road in town (absurd, I know, but what can you do?). This view does scant justice to the genuine wit that can be part and parcel of quiz night. For example, having struggled with Questions 1 to 4 above, one team's answer to Question 5 was: 'They're all wrong!'

9. A Charismatic and Witty Quizmaster

Maybe not a combination of words you were expecting to find in the same phrase, and it's true that some quizmasters can be po-faced control freaks (not the ones who run the quizzes I go to, obviously). However, the majority are decent, fair-minded and sensitive souls ('If you prick us, do we not bleed?' – Shylock in *The Merchant of Venice*) who, when the mood takes them, can even be quite funny. For example, I attended a quiz in Edinburgh where the quizmaster suddenly threw in a bonus question, namely: 'Which four Formula 1 drivers share all or part of their names with places in Scotland?' A number of the teams quickly ticked off Lewis Hamilton and Stirling Moss, and, after a little more thought, Eddie Irvine. However, no one could get the fourth driver and in the end the quizmaster put us out of our misery thus: 'The driver you are missing is Ayrton Senna.' To collective cries of 'Whaaaaat???' he went on: 'Try saying "Ayr Town Centre" in a Glasgow accent!'

10. Winning

Great as all these other things are, nothing tops that magical moment when your team is announced as the ultimate winner. At last you can dispense with your 'game face' as you bask in the satisfaction of a job well done, safe in the knowledge that all your 'hard work' has paid off. You sit back contentedly as the stress falls away, grinning stupidly around you in a state of pure euphoria that, without doubt, rivals that of the identically-named 2012 Eurovision Song Contest Winner, sung by Loreen (representing Sweden), which notched up a staggering 372 points.

10 KEY FACTS
ICELAND

1. Reykjavik – world's most northerly capital (means 'smoky bay')
2. Currency – Krona; flag – red/white Nordic cross on blue background
3. Separated from Greenland by Denmark Strait
4. Major geysers – Geysir and Strokkur
5. Most notorious volcano – Eyjafjallajökull (exact spelling not important)
6. Parliament – Althing
7. Fought 'Cod Wars' with UK in 1950s and 70s
8. Famous pop musicians – Björk, Sigur Rós and Of Monsters and Men
9. Bobby Fischer, chess champion, granted citizenship in 2005
10. Sacked former Atomic Kitten singer Kerry Katona in 2009 following rumours of alleged cocaine use.

GUESS WHAT?

PUB QUIZ FREQUENCY

Based on a 2007 survey of Scottish pubs conducted by dpquiz.co.uk, Thursday (31%) is the most popular day of the week for holding pub quizzes, followed by Sunday and Monday (18%), Tuesday (15%), Wednesday (12%), Friday (6%) and finally Saturday when none of the pubs surveyed ran a quiz.

NOT SO GREAT THINGS ABOUT PUB QUIZZES

If aliens were to drop in on a pub quiz, they might be forgiven for assuming they'd landed in a library or cathedral rather than a place of entertainment, given the prevailing atmosphere of devout concentration. But all is not what it seems and, were they to listen in more closely, they might form a different impression. For a start, they'd probably hear the odd whispered but urgent utterance along the lines of: 'Wait. It's on the tip of my tongue. No, bugger! It's gone again!', or: 'Don't be daft! It's definitely not her. She may have appeared in *Emmerdale* but no way was she ever in *Corrie*!' or maybe a hissed: 'All right! Well done! But keep your voice down, moron!'

The thing is, the pub quiz is a contest and we Brits are highly competitive, however laid-back we may appear. Therefore, beneath the veneer of genteel tranquillity, people are getting stressed and tempers are fraying, revealing some of the less edifying traits of the pub quizzer. Here are ten of them.

1. Taking things far too seriously, and then complaining that other teams are taking things far too seriously.

2. Emitting artificially loud peals of laughter about nothing that is remotely funny, in order to try and disguise the fact that they are taking things far too seriously.

3. Uttering the word 'easy' in a stage whisper when they happen by chance to have stumbled upon the answer to some highly obscure question that the other teams are struggling with.

4. During any break in proceedings, assuming that reciting the names of the 50 US States, including their capitals and nicknames, is an adequate substitute for adult conversation.

5. Loudly congratulating each other when they figure out a challenging answer, then shushing other teams who do the same.

6. Getting increasingly narked with everyone, about everything, as the evening progresses.

7. Clapping themselves when they are announced as the winners.

   Or, if they don't win ...

8. Saying they didn't mind losing, only for their true feelings to be betrayed by their burning cheeks, rictus grins and inability to make eye contact with the winning team.

9. Complaining that their defeat is somehow incontrovertible proof that the quiz is going downhill.

10. Announcing that they might give it a miss next week, whereas the truth is that hell will freeze over before that ever happens.

The Psychology of the Pub Quiz Winner

What does the term 'hardcore pub quizzer' conjure up in your mind? Is it the image of someone you'd cross the road to avoid, or who you'd hate to sit next to on a bus? These archetypal quiz nuts are usually middle-aged blokes who hunt in packs, don't smile a lot and share an intense dislike of vegetables.

Guys like this look as if they could do with some vitamin D supplements, an even shave and a symmetrical haircut. Typically, these men are employed either in IT or as invoice clerks, watch non-league football and are usually called Norman. They are unlikely to be married (unless to a woman called Norma). Their team name will inevitably reflect some weak attempt at humour, e.g. Norman's Conquest or The Stormin' Normans, but to the rest of the pub they are simply Norman and his No-Mates. They tend to occupy the corner table, and they always seem to win. I know this sounds like an unfair generalisation but when you've been to as many pub quizzes as I have you do tend to see a lot of these stereotypes.

Why do pub quizzes hold a particular appeal for this type of man, and why are they so damned good? The answer quite simply is that a high level of quiz performance requires a mastery of facts, which is something these guys are fiercely motivated to achieve. This is because facts are passive things that (a) are capable of being mastered and (b) can't threaten them. So the pub quiz provides an opportunity for the hardcore quizzer to be seen as proficient at something that is completely within their control and which, for the first time in their lives, is not a solitary occupation.

So, how are you supposed to know a hardcore quizzer when you see one? For instance, what if you are recruiting to a pub quiz team but feel unable to ask anyone outright for fear of causing offence or attracting ridicule? To help solve this dilemma, here are some simple and non-invasive steps for testing whether someone might have hardcore potential:

1. Ask him what hobbies he has. If the answer involves the words 'spotting', 'collecting' or 'live-action role play', proceed to Step 2.

2. Express an interest in any aspect of his hobby, e.g. by saying something like: 'I've always wanted to understand more about the construction of the Class 303 Gresley Bogey.' If he invites you into his home, proceed to Step 3.

3. When inside his home, look out for the obvious signs – CD collection indexed alphabetically, rows of hardback files labelled 'History', 'Movies' etc. If these are present, proceed to Step 4.

4. Check out the 'smallest room in the house' – in fact, if he describes it in these terms, you may as well sign him up there and then. Now observe whether the toilet roll is positioned with the end facing away from the wall or against it, and simply turn the roll round. After your suspect has visited the SRITH himself, go back in and see if he's replaced the roll back to its original position. If he has, you will have found yourself a new team-mate, and probably a very good one at that.

This is the psychological profile of the serial quizzer – a master of inanimate objects in their home, and of infinite facts in the pub. Within their own four walls they sit there placidly, re-indexing their files and rote-learning facts, while resolutely declining to startle any passing goose. But the pub quiz turns them into crazy demons, drawing out their Superman (born Kal-El on the planet Krypton) from their Clark Kent (works for the *Daily Planet*) or, if you prefer, their Mr Hyde (Edward) from their Dr Jekyll (Henry).

Having recruited this quizzing behemoth, a worrying thought may occur to you. How can you compete with people like this, or even add anything to a quiz team with them in it? Well, here's where this book will help, by setting out a step-by-step improvement programme for you, culminating in pub quiz supremacy.

Firstly, however, it is necessary to establish a baseline – i.e. the raw material that we are working with in terms of your quizzing potential – so let's start with a simple test to assess whether you possess the innate personality traits of the hardcore quizzer. Consider which of the following statements apply to you:

- I don't drive because I find it scary that I cannot control what everyone else on the road is doing.

- I find social interaction difficult because no one else seems to know anything about diesel locomotives.

- I'd rather have a job that involves dealing with things (e.g. invoices or computing code) rather than people, because things don't give me a hard time.

- I refuse to engage with my emotions because I can't get the stains out afterwards.

If three or more of those statements apply to you, and you are not a regular quizzer, then you are missing your vocation and should urgently consider changing your name by deed-poll to Norman (or Norma) in the unlikely event that you are not already thus named. You clearly have massive pub-quiz potential and this book will help you realise it.

But don't be too concerned if this is not you. As we saw earlier, a number of other types of people are to be found at the pub quiz – maybe people like you – and they too can become top players. Let's take a look at the underlying psychology of their quizzing addiction.

Other Quizzing 'Types'

The middle-aged couples
It's quite possible that our middle-aged couples are nothing more than Normans who have found their Normas, in which case we need dwell no further. But if this is not the case, we must dig a little deeper, particularly into the minds of the men.

To all intents and purposes the lifestyles of these guys will be unremarkable. They will drive mid-range family saloons, hold down successful careers, be emotionally intelligent and interact well socially. Their only blemish will be that they have suddenly taken up pub quizzing. And the reason that the whole group entered the pub smiling and chatting away is that their wives are absolutely delighted with this turn of events. You see, every man has the right to a mid-life crisis, and getting into pub quizzing is one of its very mildest forms. After all, think how much worse it could be – he could be driving a Harley-Davidson around Ealing or insisting on going clubbing with his 19-year-old daughter and her mates, dressed in his finest chinos. For families like these, the pub quiz is a godsend – the men are fulfilled and their wives are relieved.

The youngsters (possibly students)
Next in were the young guys, accompanied by the odd girl, and these groups fall into two categories – (a) the studious ones and (b) the bright young things.

The studious group, usually with a limited or nonexistent female presence, are in fact precociously earnest quizzers. Even at their tender years they have figured out that life's going to be one huge pile of doo-doo, and are already battening down the hatches so they don't have to deal with anything animate. Quite simply, they are tomorrow's serial quiz winners, or wannabe Normans. They may even choose a team name which references that of their hardcore heroes e.g. The Norman Non-quest, thus becoming the pub quiz equivalent of tribute acts such as Björn Again, Fake That or Ironic Maiden.

Top 10 Quiz Songs

1. 'Do They Know It's Quizmas?'
2. 'Know More Heroes'
3. 'Joker Face'
4. 'Quiz You Nights'
5. 'Brimful of Answers'
6. 'Tie-break Hotel'
7. 'Quiz You Like Crazy'
8. 'Zorba The Geek'
9. 'Happy Dork'
10. 'It Started With a Quiz'

The other type of younger group, the bright young things, will have a more balanced gender mix and are all likely to be unfeasibly good-looking. They will consist of hunky posh guys with Hugh Grant-style floppy hair and jutting jaws who say 'and stuff' after each sentence, or nubile young women with impossibly peachy complexions and a tendency to blurt out things like: 'Omigod!!! That round was soooo not easy!!!' These are the postmodernist quizzers, who are here strictly for the irony. They will finish last, week in week out, coolly revelling in their rubbishness. God bless 'em.

The senior citizens

Finally we observed our more elderly quizzers – men and women who are well into their seventies or beyond. What brings them to the pub quiz, aside from the fact that they may have mistakenly assumed it was Bingo Night? Well, the simple answer is that they are with their fifty-something hardcore quizzer sons. In this case it transpires that some Normans are housetrained to a point where a certain type of selfless octogenarian parent is prepared to be seen in public with them. This bestows upon the Normans a veneer of social conformity, only for this to be betrayed by their lack of emotional responsiveness, rather like the replicants in *Bladerunner* (made in 1982 and based on 'Do Androids Dream of Electric Sheep?' by Philip K(indred) Dick).

A Sociological Perspective

If you find the psychological paradigm a touch stereotypical, you may prefer the sociological alternative, which assumes that pub quizzers simply reflect the social hierarchy of early twenty-first century Britain. From this model we can start to draw out some of the moral and tactical elements of pub quizzing, with reference to the three main social strata.

Greedy bankers

The topmost stratum comprises the pub quizzing equivalent of greedy bankers. These are the most successful teams who are ruthlessly avaricious in their pursuit of pub quiz riches. They arbitrage the highest possible score out of the embattled quizmaster by aggressive trading: 'Look! The answer was the Sugababes and we put The Smiths; surely, that's worth a half point for the word "The".'

They are not averse to a spot of white-collar crime – nothing so vulgar as blatant cheating with their Smartphones during the quiz, but rather more subtle ruses such as coming to the pub armed with a list of the key events of the last seven days for surreptitious reference during the Current Affairs round – more a case of defeat avoidance than evasion, or so they'd have you believe.

The amoral underclass

At the other end of the spectrum lurks the amoral underclass. These are the rioters and looters who will employ any means to win. They swan in (to the Swan Inn?) from the outlying estates with their Smartphones, and then quite openly cheat their way to the first prize of a bottle of the house wine. And they are so shameless that they choose not to use the wine for the purpose intended (i.e. vinegar in the case of white wine and de-rusting agent in the case of red) but instead brazenly indulge in substance abuse by actually drinking the stuff, swigging it straight from the bottle while perched menacingly on the wall outside the pub at 1.30am.

The squeezed middle

In between we encounter the 'squeezed middle' – the silent majority of honest folk who toil away each week, learning their facts and memorising their lists in order to try and better themselves for the sake of their families.

These people are scrupulously fair, they never give the quizmaster a hard time and are unfailingly friendly, courteous and smiley. Where does all this get them? It gets them to eighth place. Every week. And for their troubles they are rewarded by patronising remarks from the quizmaster about what troopers they are and how great it is to see them here again. Yet still they come back, showing a selfless devotion to the quizzing cause, because, like so many other people, they just can't stay away.

PUB QUIZZES — AN INTERNATIONAL PHENOMENON?

Pub quizzes can also be found in many of the major countries of the world, but they are usually run by British ex-pats rather than being a feature of the native culture. However, in some English-speaking regions like Australasia and North America, trivia evenings of an indigenous nature are becoming an increasingly common occurrence.

Taking the USA as an example, Wikipedia's Pub Quiz entry reports that some 2,000 events are held across the States each week. This is based on data provided by TriviaReviews.com which includes a map showing the distribution of pub quizzes throughout the USA. Unsurprisingly, this suggests that most quizzes take place in the major conurbations such as New York, Los Angeles and Chicago, with relatively few being held in more rural parts.

However, I can now divulge the results of some exclusive research of my own which presents a somewhat different picture because I have in fact unearthed the existence of a quizzing belt which runs down the spine of the country, stretching from North and South Dorkota along the Quizzouri and Quizzissippi valleys through to Jokerlahoma. Moreover, I have conducted a thorough and objective analysis of the relative quizzing abilities among different states which reveals that the most successful participants are from Winnesota and Winsconsin while the wooden spoon (or rather the consolation sweets) goes to Lose-ianna and Alas-score.

Either way, it is clear that pub quizzing is becoming big business across the pond, though some might say that this is no great surprise given that the landmass was discovered by Quiztopher Columbus.

HOW THE PUB EVOLVED

The first 'pubs' appeared in Britain during Roman times. Known as 'tabernae', they served food and wine, displaying vine leaves outside to advertise their trade.

During the Saxon era ale was brewed by many people, and those who brewed the best ale sold it more widely. When they also opened their homes up as places in which to drink it, the alehouse came into being. During the Medieval era, as water supplies became polluted by industries and the impacts of an increased population, ale became the only safe drink whereupon alehouses took on a more permanent role.

As society became more mobile during the later Middle Ages due to the expanding woollen trade and the advent of pilgrimages, roadside inns became established, providing food and accommodation as well as ale.

As England prospered during the reign of the Tudors, larger towns took root and were served by taverns which provided places of leisure for the emerging middle classes, while the alehouse remained as a place of necessity for the poorer folk.

During the Stuart era, wars with France resulted in a ban on importing French wine and brandy, and the distilling of gin was encouraged, leading to its widespread availability in 'gin houses'. The detrimental effect of gin on the population resulted in legislation in 1830 to encourage more beer brewing, resulting in many thousands of new 'beer houses'. These, together with the surviving and more ornate 'gin palaces', taverns and inns, saw the emergence of the public house as we would recognise it today.

NOW TEST YOURSELF

EASY-PEASY

1. What type of garment is a Niqab?

2. Which adjective did Ronald Reagan use to describe the Soviet Empire in a 1982 speech?

3. What word can come before aid, wire and long?

4. In the title of the 1930 Evelyn Waugh novel, which word goes before 'Bodies'?

5. What is the connection between the above answers?

(Answers on page 127)

In summary, pub quizzes attract all sorts of folk – young and old, male and female, rich and poor, weird and normal – and I have tried to highlight the key reasons for this phenomenon, drawing on meticulously conducted psycho-sociological research based on a few nights down the pub chatting to strangers and drunk friends. But whatever your personality type or socio-economic grouping, if you want to become a pub quiz winner you will need to submit yourself to an exhaustive programme of self-improvement. That's where I come in.

READ ON, we've got a lot more to get through yet ...

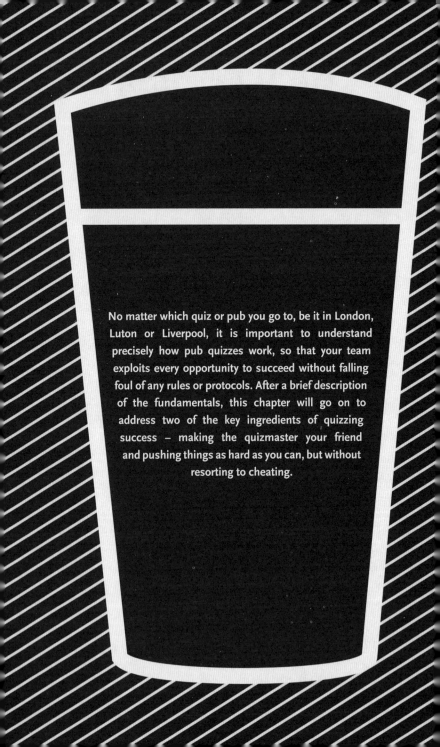

No matter which quiz or pub you go to, be it in London, Luton or Liverpool, it is important to understand precisely how pub quizzes work, so that your team exploits every opportunity to succeed without falling foul of any rules or protocols. After a brief description of the fundamentals, this chapter will go on to address two of the key ingredients of quizzing success – making the quizmaster your friend and pushing things as hard as you can, but without resorting to cheating.

LET'S GET QUIZZICAL

MAKING THE QUIZ WORK FOR YOU

WHAT ARE PUB QUIZZES?

Let's start with the basics.

'A PUB QUIZ IS A QUIZ ... THAT TAKES PLACE IN A PUB.'

A small entry fee is normally charged to participants, who organise themselves into teams, typically between two and six players. The teams are then asked a series of questions and they write down their answers, which are marked and totalled, the winner being the team with the highest number of correct answers.

The event is presided over by a quizmaster who reads the questions, gives out the answers, adjudicates on any queries and announces the final placings. The quizmaster may collect the answer sheets and mark them himself, or the sheets may be swapped between teams for marking. A 'tie-break' question may be deployed to determine the winner in the event of the highest score being shared by two or more teams.

Pub quiz questions tend to comprise a combination of general knowledge plus some more specialist facts, topped with a bunch of complete and utter trivia. They will be of varying degrees of difficulty, and will typically number between 50 and 100 in total.

Questions are usually grouped into rounds, which are often themed by subject or in some other way. Teams may be asked to nominate a 'Joker' round, meaning their score for that round will be doubled. Handout rounds (e.g. containing photos of famous people to be identified) may also be distributed for teams to complete either during the quiz or at the halfway point, where there is usually a short break to allow time for drinks to be replenished or for snacks (invariably beige, pork-related or crispy in nature) to be served and eaten.

The winners, and maybe the runners-up, will receive a prize in the form of a modest amount of cash or perhaps a bottle of wine or a round of drinks. A small (and in no way patronising whatsoever at all) consolation prize such as a bag of sweets may also be awarded to the team finishing last.

And that's it really, apart from two essential rules:

1. Assuming the quiz is halfway decent, everyone will enjoy a terrific evening's entertainment

2. The winning team will be captained by a serious-looking middle-aged man, probably called Norman

Rule 2 may be broken, but only by people who follow this book right through to the very last page, digesting its contents line by line. So let's make a start by tackling a vital topic – how to get the quizmaster on your side.

THE CULT OF THE QUIZMASTER

'So, layeesangennelmen, we're now approaching the end of tonight's proceedings,' s(pr)ays the quizmaster. *'The scores are going to be close, so pay particular attention to the last question.'*

Your team is on edge. For the first time in weeks you are ahead going into the last round. You'd lost ground early doors as usual to The Stormin' Normans on the clever people's rounds like Geography and Science, but you'd played your Joker on the Music round and the gamble had paid off. For once, the quizmaster has turned to his teenage daughter for the musical clips so you'd had a bit of Adele and Rihanna rather than Cilla Black and Clodagh Rodgers.

'Here is the question,' continues the quizmaster. 'How many arms does a squid possess?' (He always talks with an annoying nasal twang, like the one used by police detectives when giving media briefings, such that 'possess' becomes 'peauzzzessss'). 'That's easy – it's ten,' you exclaim triumphantly to your team. 'I think we're home and hosed.' You attempt to say this in a whisper but the sound hisses around the pub because your voice is crackling with anticipation. Angry glares are shot in your direction, particularly by the Normans, who appear to be involved in a heated discussion. However, you barely notice because you are sure that you have WON.

You float through the next 15 minutes in a bubble of serenity, while the papers are swapped and the answers read out. But then your bubble is abruptly burst by the quizmaster announcing that a squid in fact has eight arms. Cue stunned silence, broken only by the sounds of whooping Normans. 'Eight?' you exclaim in disbelief. 'Yes,' responds the quizmaster, smirking (despite the smirking ban). 'Strictly speaking, they peauzzzessss eight arms plus two tentacles. I did advise you to pay particular attention to the question.'

Your team is aghast. 'Oh, for goodness' sake! That is so infuriating. Why has he got to try and be so clever all the time? He'll be disappearing up his own anorak if he's not careful. The quiz is not all about him. He's supposed to be here to provide us with a good evening's entertainment, not to show off his nitpicky knowledge. I'll kick him in *his* tentacles if he comes anywhere near me.'

Understanding your quizmaster, and what makes him or her tick, is one of the most vital elements of pub quiz success because there are points to be gained if you know how to pull his or her strings. At this point I am going to dispense with the 'his and her' nonsense – quizmasters are always blokes because women, generally speaking, have far better things to do with their time (like posting on Facebook about what they had for their afters).

It is often said that people fall into one of two camps when it comes to quizmasters – there are those who don't like them and those who can't stand them. However, there are two sides to every coin, so let's try to adopt a more balanced perspective by taking a look at some of the best and worst characteristics of the quizmaster (or in other words, the good and the bad of the ugly).

TRAITS OF A GOOD QUIZMASTER

1. Showmanship

Quizmasters should be extroverts, or at least they should be capable of projecting an extrovert side to their personality (though not in that cheesy '1980s Saturday night variety show host' kind of way). They should be confident individuals who are comfortable speaking in public. In fact, they probably need to be bi-polar – introvert when doing the meticulous research involved in preparing the quiz and extrovert when delivering it. This is not an easy combination and the ones who can carry this off are really quite impressive individuals.

It's important to draw a distinction between showmanship and showing off, because no one likes a smartarse. Quizmasters who ask questions like: 'Translate the Latin phrase: *Cras credemus, hodie nihil*,' (answer: tomorrow we believe, but not today) need to understand that they are not Stephen Fry and this ain't *QI*. It's the *Canis et Anas* (Dog and Duck) on a Thursday night and the punters (*hoi polloi* – which is Greek rather than Latin) will soon be getting restless. They won't be impressed by any meretricious display of cultural superiority, and will quickly conclude that the quizmaster is simply a *Caput Todgeri* (knob-head).

2. Likeability

It's probably stating the blindingly obvious, but it really helps if the quizmaster is a likeable individual who is capable of building good relationships with the teams. Part of that is having a good memory for faces, names and characters. For example, if a team gives a spectacularly bad or brilliant answer to a question one week, the quizmaster can refer back to it when a similar situation subsequently arises. It works to the quizmaster's advantage if they can establish some banter with the teams or with the bar staff ('That one must be easy – even Craig knows the answer'). Forging strong relationships with the teams should reduce the likelihood of jarring challenges from the floor and make them easier to deal with, should they arise.

3. Humour

One of the quizmaster's main weapons is what appears in the lonely hearts ads as a GSOH (was I really the last person in the country to realise that this doesn't stand for 'Gas Central Heating'?). Being able to make his audience laugh and having the ability to laugh at himself are key attributes for getting teams onside, so that any difficult adjudications will be accepted with good grace. A witty or self-deprecating response to a bit of banter from the floor can be a major asset on the part of the quizmaster.

I know of one quizmaster who had the contestants in the palm of his hand from the off. His quiz formed the social element of a company jolly (er, sorry, team-building away-day) and was attended by a sizeable contingent of junior staff plus a few senior managers. The quizmaster began the quiz as follows:

'Question 1: What is your company's mission statement?' This was greeted by a combination of earnest scribbling among the senior people and audible groans and rolled eyes on the part of the more junior staff. The quizmaster let the situation run for about 15 seconds, before saying: 'Only joking. Question 1 really is: What colour is Noddy's hat!?' As Renée Zellweger put it in *Jerry Maguire*, he had them at hello (well, most of them anyway).

4. Strength of personality

Quizmasters should have forceful personalities because they do need to have what it takes to work a room, so shoe-gazers need not apply. However, they must avoid becoming too hectoring (as was the attitude apparently adopted by William Gladstone towards Queen Victoria, who said of him: 'He always addresses me as if I were a public meeting').

Likeability and humour will help quizmasters avoid too much aggro, but there will sometimes be one or two difficult individuals in a room full of quizzers, and the odd incident may arise where diplomacy is not enough to diffuse things. On such occasions a firm but friendly put-down may be required, as with the case of the Test batsman who, responding to persistent 'sledging' to the effect that he was overweight, replied: 'It's because every time I sleep with your wife, she gives me a biscuit.' OK, maybe not quite that brutal, but on occasion a forceful response may be needed to maintain an element of control.

5. Clarity

Clarity is another vital weapon in the quizmaster's armoury. It is important that quizzers are absolutely clear on matters like how many marks will be awarded for each question and precisely what type of answer is being sought. A good quizmaster should state each question clearly and then repeat it during the round while inviting requests for further repeats at the end. He should use the mic sensibly, and not bellow into it thereby soaking the nearest five teams in phlegm like Roy Hattersley's *Spitting Image* puppet. And he should maintain an appropriate pace – not so fast that teams are struggling to keep up ('Oi, mate, you got a train to catch?') but equally not so pedestrian that the quiz loses momentum.

HOW TO EXPLOIT THE QUIZMASTER

What does all this mean for teams who are looking to maximise their points tally? Well, there are obvious benefits to be gained from establishing a good rapport with the quizmaster – both parties will enjoy the occasion more, and your team's challenges will be less likely to fall on deaf ears. So when you say something like: 'The answer is Agatha Christie but we put Linford Christie – is it half a mark for surname?' you might just get away with it. Let's now review a couple of these traits and examine how you can turn them to your advantage.

Showmanship: a showman looks for people to feed off who will give as good as they get, so your team should in turn exude confident and friendly vibes, and establish plenty of eye contact with the quizmaster. The occasional cry of 'Excellent question!' should help no end, as will 'Good call!' when he makes a tricky adjudication, particularly if it goes against the Normans, in which case you should also compliment him on his steadfast refusal to be intimidated by a hailstorm of half-eaten cocktail sausages.

Humour is another quite easy trait to exploit, by use of some well-chosen banter. For example, if the quizmaster asks: 'What is the only mammal that lives as a parasite?' (he'll be looking for the answer of vampire bat) simply shout out: 'My teenage son!' and you'll make an immediate friend, and quite possibly gain a bonus point for your efforts. Or in response to the question: 'What is the capital of Ireland?' try saying: 'About ten Euros these days, mate, innit?' and you may earn a spot prize for your wit (and your ability to recycle other people's jokes).

And a little flattery as you leave the pub never goes amiss if you want to increase your team's stock with the quizmaster: 'Cracking quiz tonight – you must have put in a load of work to come up with such interesting questions.' This will carry added weight if you can still manage to say this after your team has lost (although you may find you require dental surgery to un-grit your teeth if they are still locked in position the following morning).

But for every charismatic and winning quizmaster, there is always the odd Alan Partridge or David Brent, so let's take a look at some of the characteristics of the less capable practitioners.

TRAITS OF A BAD QUIZMASTER

1. Being a 'Self-Styled Character'

Beware the quizmaster who is a 'self-styled character' (SSC). This is the sort of guy who rocks up wearing a silly wig or Groucho Marx moustache and glasses, or perhaps a Kiss Me Quick hat. If you are struggling to envisage the type of person I'm describing, think Smashie and Nicey – we're talking 1970s Radio 1 DJs or current local radio presenters.

The thing I've noticed with these guys is that humour is fine when *they* are delivering it or, to put it more accurately, when they're attempting to do so. However, if someone else tries to get in on the act, the SSC can get quite ratty.

I remember one occasion when I actually got told off three times by an SSC before the quiz had even started, after he came round the tables to take our team names. The fact that each table already had a number had led us to assume that nothing more was needed so I said, 'Table Twelve,' to which the SSC replied: 'Come on, this is a fun quiz. At least make the effort to think up an amusing name.' Suitably chastened, I delved into my reservoir of funny quiz team names and came up with one of the old classics for tripping up the quizmaster, 'Ken Dodd's Dad's Dog's Dead', to which he snapped back, 'No, no, no! You can't expect me to say that. That's far too long. Come up with something better than that for goodness' sake.' So shorter, but in the same spirit, I offered 'And In Third Place' to which he retorted: 'Now you're being stupid. That's just going to confuse people.' 'Table Twelve' it was then.

The moral here is to go along with whatever the SSC says, laugh at their inanities and maintain a matey grin as you challenge for any extra half-points, and you might just get away with it (as a bonus you may even come away with a T-shirt bearing the inscription: 'You don't have to be mad to be me but it helps'). Quiz-tastic, mate!

2. Fussiness

As we saw with the squid example, a certain type of quizmaster can be extremely picky. A classic indicator of an impending fussy turn is when the quizmaster follows a question with an ominous little rider (often uttered with heightened nasality to show he means business) such as: '... and I need yieew to be as specific as yieew can here', or '... and I need all three elements of the answer here'. The trick in this case is to resist at all costs the temptation to reply: 'Here are three elements for you, mate – Potassium, Nobelium and Boron. Check the symbols.'

3. Fascism

We all know the type – little man, bristly moustache, short fuse and totally certain of his own moral rectitude. The first rule for teams here is not to attempt *any* kind of humour, because this kind of guy is liable to rush over to your table, haul you out of your chair, slam you against the speakers and ram your head into the mic stand before frogmarching you out of the pub. The best policy is to do exactly what he says and never challenge him. Although your team may not gain any extra marks, other teams who are less prudent are likely to find themselves suffering a 40-point deduction for gross insubordination.

4. Pomposity

This really is the David Brent character – totally up himself, no self-awareness and zero sense of humour. He'll say things like: 'There are only three rules to my quizzes: Rule 1: the quizmaster is always right. Rule 2: the quizmaster is always right. Rule 3: the quizmaster is always right.' In my experience, the only possible chance you have of getting extra marks off such a man is to interject at this point: 'Where I come from there's a fourth rule – the quizmaster is always right.'

5. Indulging his pet-likes

Quizmaster: 'Next question: Name all five ingredients of a Mojito cocktail.'

Now you may think to yourself that this is an unfair question. Asking for one is fair enough – maybe the main alcoholic ingredient or mixer. Two is pushing it, and anything more is just plain ludicrous. But here is how not to respond: 'All five? You're 'avin' a laugh, aren't you? You'll end up with a Rusty Nail through your Tom Collins if you're not careful.'

Tricky one, this. One idea is to have a gentle word in his shell-like to suggest that he might be getting things a little out of proportion. Another approach is to get to know him better, perhaps by way of a slow screw against the wall, and learn what his other favourite subjects are, and then start revising (whereupon you will learn that the ingredients of a Mojito are white rum, sugar, lime juice, sparkling water and mint).

And that's all you need to know about the quizmaster. In short, if you learn how to stroke his ego (and you may find you don't have too much trouble locating it) then your team should be able to blag its way to some critical extra points.

A WORD ABOUT CHEATING

And that word is 'DON'T!' Just to keep you on your toes, let's try you with an anagram. The clue is: 'People who use their mobile phones to cheat at pub quizzes', and the letters are NARK SEW.

It is important that teams are clear on what constitutes cheating, lest what they believe to be innocuous behaviour results in the humiliation of being docked ten points or being asked to leave the pub. This section will guide you through this moral minefield in order to help ensure that your team remains on the right side of the line.

The most obvious example of cheating these days involves the illegal use of Smartphones. Anyone who does this is an unscrupulous git, but also pretty thick, because intelligent people simply don't think like that – why not just get the words 'I am a stupid person' tattooed onto their foreheads to save time? But have you ever gained an advantage from overhearing another team's answer to a question you were struggling with? I certainly have, along with most other quizzers, I imagine. Is that a form of cheating? By the strictest definition it probably is, but it's hardly a hanging offence, otherwise pub quizzes would have died out long ago.

Cheating encompasses a spectrum of behaviour, and the thing to know is where to draw the line between cheating and gamesmanship. The latter – gaining an advantage by dubious but not illegal means – will be covered in the next chapter, but the remainder of this chapter will address what I have termed 'bad' and 'good' cheating, and how that can be prevented by the savvy quizmaster.

Bad Cheating

This involves gaining an unfair advantage by means which are plainly wrong by any reasonable definition. The classic examples of bad cheating are, of course, illicit use of mobile phones, either to Google answers or to text friends for them, or popping outside to phone a friend on the pretext of a fag break.

Repeated trips to the toilet during the quiz can also be suspicious (though equally they can be perfectly innocent – perhaps male quizzers over the age of 50 should be asked to complete and sign a Prostate Issues Statement Sheet before the quiz starts, or would that be taking things too far?) Further examples of 'bad' cheating are forming syndicates with nearby teams to exchange answers, or surreptitiously copying down the answers of unsuspecting neighbours. Or simply where teams bump up their score after their answer sheet has been marked and returned, or fail to correct significant over-marking.

Many articles on how to prevent cheating stress the need to devise questions that are hard to Google, such as: 'Which pop song title can be paraphrased as "Desist from glancing over your shoulder in a state of irritation"('Don't Look Back In Anger'). Actually, I've just tried Googling this and got 'Immanuel Kant – Perpetual Peace' (which was of course by Blur rather than Oasis), so that certainly does the trick. But while this is fine in principle, it merely serves to complicate the already onerous task of putting a quiz together. It is also incredibly restrictive in that literally millions of perfectly good questions can't be used because they are cheatable. It's as if the cheats are calling the shots and totally cramping the quizmaster's style.

All, however, is not lost, and publicans and quizmasters have at their disposal a variety of superior measures to put a stop to such nonsense, as examined below:

Making the prizes modest

Some pubs offer way too much money for winning – maybe £100 or more – which is sufficient to attract the cheats. If this size of pot results from a good turnout of players each paying an entrance fee of, say, £2, the pub should simply reduce the charge or allocate most of the takings to a worthy charity (such as the first-time authors' benevolent fund).

Making it clear that cheating will not be tolerated

A few words up front from the quizmaster, including asking people to put their phones away, are a friendly but timely reminder that cheating will not be tolerated. Or, better still, an introduction from the publican him/herself to that effect will carry an additional air of authority, with the added implication that any transgressors may expect a visit from the scary-looking regulars in the public bar, tooled up with pool cues and a fistful of darts.

Walking the room

If the quizmaster walks around the tables as he delivers each question, Smartphone cheating becomes almost impossible. Since PA systems with static mics prevent this, many pubs and quizmasters have invested in radio mics, leaving them free to walk among the teams without having to strain their vocal cords (as a bonus, some radio mics are also capable of picking up mobile phone signals!).

Speedy marking

Marking after each round will minimise the time available for cheating, as well as enabling a running tally to be maintained throughout the evening, thereby adding to the excitement. At the very least, answer sheets should be collected twice during the quiz – once at the halfway point and again at the end, to prevent an extensive window for potential Googling and/or collusion while the food is being eaten.

Room layout

Of course, the layout of the pub is what it is, so if there are a bunch of alcoves where teams will be out of the quizmaster's sight, there is more opportunity to cheat. However, an effective counter-measure is to designate a central area for the quiz (which will have the added benefit of preserving some cosy seats for non-quizzers, well away from the crazies).

Signal jammers

Tempting as it may be for publicans or quizmasters to use signal jammers to prevent Smartphone cheating, they are illegal because they prevent contact in an emergency. However, some rural pubs still have a limited mobile signal, or none at all, which gives them an inbuilt advantage in the war against cheating.

Top 10 Songs for Quiz Cheats

1. 'Cheaty Cheaty Bang Bang'
2. 'I Want Your Text'
3. 'Blood On The Quizfloor'
4. 'A Little Less Collaboration'
5. 'Cheaky Cheater'
6. 'The Boogie Woogie Google Boy From Company B'
7. 'Every Text You Make (I'll Be Watching You)'
8. 'All Right Now'
9. 'You're (a) Cheating Tart'
10. 'Mi Cheato Latino'

Dealing With Cheating

If a landlord or quizmaster does catch someone cheating, it's best to try to diffuse the situation humorously – maybe via a warning or points deduction in the first instance. Repeat offences should result in expulsion from the quiz, plus further punishment such as being forced to watch ten episodes of *The Jeremy Kyle Show* (where they will probably spot some of their mates).

'Good' Cheating

Exploiting visual clues

Question 1: In which year was the Kronenbourg brewery founded? (cue: rush to buy a drink)

Question 2: On a dartboard, which number lies between 6 and 15? (cue: rush for the public bar toilets)

Question 3: What is inscribed around the edge of a two-pound coin? (cue: rush back to the bar to provide a plausible pretext for taking money out of pockets and purses)

To many people, this is the acceptable face of cheating – improvising an answer by the opportunistic exploitation of handy props or visual clues. There's nothing too heinous here, and it's certainly not in the same league as some of the 'bad' cheating we encountered earlier, but the situation needn't arise if the quizmaster simply avoids this type of question. Let's look at some more instances of 'good' cheating.

Bringing lists into the pub

If, each week, the quizmaster tends to ask the same type of question, e.g. Kings and Queens and their dates, some players may become tempted to run off a full list for discreet reference during the quiz (the sheet can easily be passed off as a piece of scrap paper that the player will use for making notes or suggestions during the quiz). Take a look at this crib sheet:.

*w12h1sh2r1JOh3e123r2h456e45r3h78e6jgm1EL1j1c1OCRCc2j2w3/
m2ag1234w4ve7g5e8g6EL2
gwja-tjjma-jmojqa-ajmvb-Wih(d)jt-jpzt(d)-mffp-jbal(a)(16)-ajoug-
rhjg(a)ca**gc**-bh**gc**-wm(a)tr-wtww-wah(d)cc-hhfr(d)-htde-jk(a)(35)ljrn(r)
gfjc-rrgb-wcgwb-bo*

In this example above the first two lines list all the British monarchs since 1066 in abbreviated form. The remainder details the US presidents – note the bracketed clues indicating the numbers of the more famous ones as well as highlighting those who died in office (d), were assassinated (a) or resigned (r). The bold '**gc**' indicates that Grover Cleveland was the only president to have held non-consecutive terms of office.

In the same vein, jotting down a few names and events from the week's news onto a sheet of paper and taking it into the pub can help a team gain extra points in the Current Affairs round. In either case the offending teams would argue that they've had the presence of mind to anticipate the question so it's a cunning and legitimate tactic, whereas to many this is simply cheating. Either way, it can be prevented by the quizmaster varying the format a little each week.

NOW TEST YOURSELF

EASY-ISH

1. Who was Prisoner 46664 of Robben Island?

2. In Greek Mythology, whose prophecies were doomed to be ignored?

3. What was the name of Roy Rogers' horse?

4. Which parts of a pig are the same as the nickname of Bolton Wanderers FC?

5. What is the connection between the above answers?

(Answers on page 127)

Googling after seeing the round names

Suppose the quizmaster were to dish out the answer sheets ten minutes before the quiz is due to start, and a team spots that there will be a round on Asian capitals? Would it be OK for them to Google a few of the more obscure ones before the quiz commences – or would that Hanoi the quizmaster? Once again, this can be avoided if round titles are not shown on the answer sheet, which illustrates the main message in this section – that cheating, whether 'good' or 'bad', can be prevented by a clued-up quizmaster.

Having dealt with the basic pub quiz rules and protocols, the rest of this book will chart a series of specific steps that, if followed assiduously, will make you and your team more effective performers. Firstly, however, I'm going to break off to do one of my pub quiz fact drills, in this case testing myself on 1990s TV crime drama series – should be a Cracker.

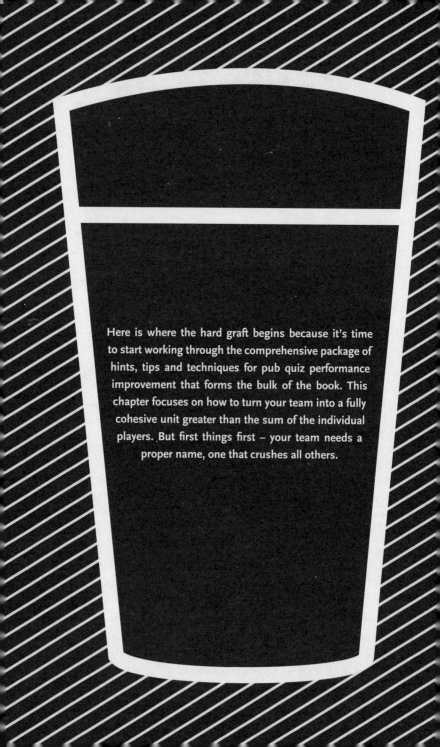

Here is where the hard graft begins because it's time to start working through the comprehensive package of hints, tips and techniques for pub quiz performance improvement that forms the bulk of the book. This chapter focuses on how to turn your team into a fully cohesive unit greater than the sum of the individual players. But first things first – your team needs a proper name, one that crushes all others.

3

ONWARD, QUIZTIAN SOLDIERS

TURNING YOUR TEAM INTO A WINNING MACHINE

TEAM NAMES

To say that pub quizzers are inventive with their names would be an understatement. Hearing the team names called out can be one of the highlights of the evening. Most quizmasters enjoy reading out a funny name and some are even prepared to reward the most inventive teams with a prize. Pub quiz team names are a perfect microcosm of the British sense of humour, and tend to fall into a handful of classic categories, as follows[3]:

Puns

My local newspaper once ran a competition to find the best pun. I sent in no fewer than ten entries, thinking that one of them was bound to win. But, do you know what, No Pun In Ten Did. *Da-dum, tsh!* We Brits just love a pun, and this is often reflected in our choice of pub quiz team names, like this lot:

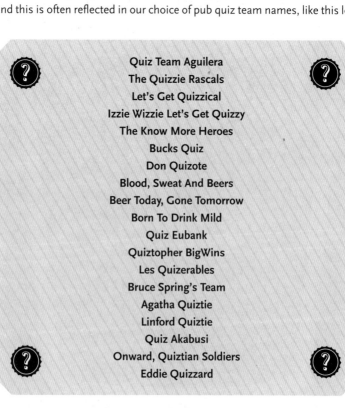

Quiz Team Aguilera
The Quizzie Rascals
Let's Get Quizzical
Izzie Wizzie Let's Get Quizzy
The Know More Heroes
Bucks Quiz
Don Quizote
Blood, Sweat And Beers
Beer Today, Gone Tomorrow
Born To Drink Mild
Quiz Eubank
Quiztopher BigWins
Les Quizerables
Bruce Spring's Team
Agatha Quiztie
Linford Quiztie
Quiz Akabusi
Onward, Quiztian Soldiers
Eddie Quizzard

I've heard that Christopher and Christine have plummeted to the bottom of the list of the UK's favourite names because anyone thus *chris*tened who goes on to achieve any kind of fame is now doomed to be the butt of atrocious punnery in over 20,000 pubs each week.

Crude

'I was walking along a narrow mountain pass when I saw a beautiful blonde coming towards me. I didn't know whether to toss myself off or block her passage.' Ah yes, good old Max Miller there, with a ripe example of bawdy British humour, a tradition that was embodied by Donald McGill with his saucy seaside postcards and then in the *Carry On* movies. And now that mantle has passed to the pub quizzer. The following names, of course, are employed as a fantastic attempt to embarrass the quizmaster when reading the names aloud, but also stand alone as delightfully tawdry jokes:

Crouching Barmaid Hidden Sausage
The Four Skins
Sausage & Gash
I'd Rather Get a 69 Than 180
Kate's Bush
My Grandmother's a Shoplifter – You Should See Her Snatch
My Wife's No Gardener, But You Should See Her Bush
My Wife Can't Wrestle But You Should See Her Box
My Dad's No Architect But You Should See His Erections
I'm Not a Gynaecologist But I Don't Mind Taking a Look
I Am a Gynaecologist But I Like To Keep My Hand In
Stop The Bus and Let My Brother Jack Off

To which one can only say: 'Ooh-er, missus.'

Anti-quizmaster

Given the mixed emotions that certain quizmasters engender in their flocks, it's no surprise that a whole raft of names have sprung up which are designed to confound or embarrass them, like these:

The Cunning Stunts
I Wish This Microphone Was a Cock
And In Last Place ...
Ken Dodd's Dad's Dog's Dead
The Cunning Linguists
The Llanfairpwllgwyngyllgogerychwyrndrobwllllantysiliogogogoch
Train-Spotting Society
Fact Hunt
The Pheasant Pluckers
The Shy Teds
The Shy Tots
Betty Swallocks
Mary Hinge
Carey Pratt and Mike Hunt

You might argue that most of these would fit equally well into the 'Crude' category, but maybe what distinguishes them is that they are designed to trick the poor old quizmaster into saying something he might live to regret. Spooner him than me.

Self-deprecation

Bob Monkhouse famously quipped, 'They laughed when I said I was going to be a comedian, but they're not laughing now!' proving that self-deprecation is another wonderful British character trait and a fertile source of quiz team names, such as:

Dazed & Confused
The Scrambled Eggheads
The Saga Louts
Blunders Never Cease
The Simple Minds
The Wooden Spoons
Norfolk'n Chance
Universally Challenged
Natural Born Losers

Surreal and Quirky

One team I know call themselves The Gobi Desert Lifeguards, which normally draws a laugh from anyone hearing the name for the first time (though not as big a laugh as when that team failed to identify either of the two countries that the Gobi Desert actually spans – China and Mongolia!). Others in the surreal and quirky genre include:

Harold Bishop's Red Speedos
Leo Sayer's Terrified Eyes
664 The Neighbour of the Beast
57 Shades Of Grey
I'm Called Brian and So Is My Wife
The Usual Suspects
The Pedants' Revolt
It's Not Big and It's Not Clever
Saving Ryan's Privates
Running With Scissors
One Wheel Short of a Unicycle
Dry Your Thighs, Mate
It's Not The Winning But The Bacon Tart

Topical

Some quizmasters encourage teams to choose a different name each week by awarding a spot prize for the best entry. For example, during that week in 2009 in which Tiger Woods was reported to have crashed his car outside his driveway while fleeing from his house, the winning entry at my pub was Crouching Tiger, Hidden Hydrant. If the task of coming up with a topical name each week seems too onerous, simply buy a copy of that day's *Sun*, because one of their sub-editors is bound to have come up with a punning headline that should do the job for you.

Tribute team names

Finally, one rather more off-beat approach is to choose a name that pays homage to another team. At one quiz I go to, where my team is called The Ministry of Truth (taken from *Nineteen Eighty-Four* by George Orwell), another team has taken to occasionally calling itself The Ministry of Guesswork by way of a tribute to us (at least I *think* it's a tribute ...). But enough of this frivolity, let's get back to the theme of winning the quiz.

TEAMWORK

There's no 'I' in 'TEAM', so the motivational gurus love to tell us, to which the correct response is: 'Yeah, but there is an 'M' and an 'E', you sanctimonious dickhead.' But in fairness, teamwork is a major factor in pub quiz success, and here are some tips.

Divvying up the subjects

One of the great things about playing in a pub quiz team is that you don't have to be an expert on every subject. For example, if you specialise in the more populist end of the spectrum, e.g. Music, TV and Film, you might be able to hook up with a couple of boffins who will pick up more serious subjects like Science, Geography and History, plus maybe a bookworm and a sports buff to complete your team.

Even if your team is coming from a base where no one is an expert on anything, you can still divvy up the subjects between you and start from scratch. However daunting that may sound, it isn't as hard as you might think to develop sufficient knowledge of a new topic for quizzing purposes (as distinct from actually knowing something about it), and a variety of techniques for achieving this will be described later in the book.

Sharing things out can also be useful in the handout rounds, particularly at quizzes where not one but six handouts are distributed at the start of the quiz, unleashing a feverish race against time. How comforting it is on such occasions to have a word-search wizard on your team, or an anagram expert, when a whole sheet of the bloody things is dished out.

Knowing each others' strengths and weaknesses
Even if you don't go the full divvying-up hog, it's still useful to discuss your respective strengths and weaknesses (or 'areas for development', as HR folk like to say), so that everyone agrees whose opinion should hold most sway when a question on a particular topic comes up.

Keeping everyone involved
Involving everyone sounds basic enough – after all, what's the point in having them on the team if their views aren't going to be heard? But when the pressure is on, there's a danger that the voices of quieter team members might be swamped by their more assertive (i.e. gobby) team-mates, even if the discussion revolves around one of their strong subjects. To avoid this, the team should collectively endorse and practise a culture of allowing everyone their say.

Equally, a 'no-blame culture' makes for a more successful team and a less stressy night out all round. The team should fully discuss any question on which there is uncertainty, with everyone signing up to the chosen answer. Then, if it turns out to be wrong, it doesn't matter who came up with the idea originally – accountability is collective. But even if one person insists on an answer that turns out to be wrong, team-mates should remember there will be other such occasions where they will be the 'culprits', so they shouldn't be getting on their high horse.

A balanced team
Having the right mix of players is absolutely key. Although a team of four or five crusty middle-aged guys is likely to be strong across many topics, there's every chance they will struggle on questions about the Kardashians or David Guetta's latest oeuvre (he's French, see) or the most recent Stella

McCartney creation or indeed which character initiated the shagfest on page 69 of *Fifty Shades of Grey*. If your team is to become as competent with this type of question as they are with 1930s steam engines, you may need to find a better mix of player, for example:

- 1 x middle-aged bloke, somewhat highbrow in taste, ideally called Norman

- 1 x middle-aged bloke, but a more 'salt of the earth' type, ideally called Norman

- 1 x middle-aged woman, ideally called Norma

- 1 x younger woman

- 1 x younger guy

What a combination this would make! It would surely have a sufficiently broad and deep knowledge of just about every conceivable topic, from Leonardo da Vinci to Leonardo DiCaprio, from Edmund Burke to Alexandra Burke, and from the Ballet Rambert to Paul Lambert.

TEAM TACTICS

Anyone new to pub quizzes may be puzzled that tactics can come into play at all – after all, you either know the answer or you don't. But as experienced quizzers will know, that's not always the case. Let's take a look at some of the tactics a team can adopt to maximise performance.

Team numbers
Size does matter, but not in the way you might think. The optimum team size is around four or five, maybe six at a push. You can get away with three or even just two if you're strong players, though you may find you come unstuck on more specialist rounds.

But at the other extreme, if you find yourselves in a pub where teams of any number are allowed, don't assume that your humble team of four will be at a disadvantage. You see, it simply isn't the case that team capability increases with size – in fact, beyond a certain point the reverse is true. For a start, many players in huge teams are only there for the beer. Moreover, any questions other than gimmes will probably generate a raucous and unfocused debate full of red herrings (which I find go quite well with the beer). So here's a tip – if you see a team of about nine people, grab the table next to them – you'll be royally entertained by all the bantering and bickering, and you may even get a few extra points from overhearing possible answers as they shout across at each other.

10 KEY FACTS
BEETHOVEN

1. Ludwig van Beethoven, German (b. Bonn), 1770–1827
2. 3rd Symphony – 'Eroica' (originally dedicated to Napoleon)
3. 5th Symphony begins 'De de de duurgh' (Fate knocking at the door)
4. 9th (final) Symphony – contains 'Ode to Joy' (words by Schiller)
5. Only opera – *Fidelio*
6. Moonlight Sonata (No. 14) dedicated to lost love
7. Only ballet – *The Creatures of Prometheus*
8. Became deaf in his twenties
9. Last words (apocryphal) – 'I shall hear in Heaven'
10. 'Roll Over Beethoven' by Chuck Berry – ELO's cover of 1973 reached No. 6.

Listen to the question

Quizmaster: Which Football League team plays its home games at Highbury?

Player 1: Dear, oh dear. What a howler. Hasn't he heard of The Emirates? Shall we tell him now or afterwards?

Player 2: Leave it until afterwards. Stick down 'Arsenal'. That'll get us the points and we'll give him some grief when he reads out the answers.

And of course the answer turns out to be Fleetwood Town who, unlike Arsenal, really are a Football League team!

It's so easy to jump to conclusions based on a selective interpretation of the question. A pub quiz classic of this type is: 'Who was the last prime minister not to have a wife?' This question certainly did for my team when we first heard it, as we quickly ticked our way down the list of male PMs and emerged triumphantly at Edward Heath, only to experience a collective 'duhh' moment when the answers were read out, because Margaret Thatcher never had a wife either! It is helpful to designate someone with the job of saying: 'Have we missed anything obvious?' when questions seem surprisingly simple.

Trust your first instinct

If you are 90 per cent certain of the answer that first pops into your head, stick with it unless there are some extremely persuasive arguments to the contrary. By all means be receptive to alternative suggestions from team-mates – after all, they may prove that you're barking up the wrong tree – but don't budge unless you become pretty sure that your first thought was incorrect. If it turns out that you're consistently wrong, accept that your judgement is crap and move on. But otherwise, you should continue to trust your first instinct.

Extracting answers from the tip of your tongue

If you find yourself mired in anomia hell and can't quite dredge an answer out, tell your team what you're thinking – maybe what the word sounds like or begins with – so they can try and help you. For example, if something's telling you that the answer begins with an 'E', team-mates can go through the alphabet – Ea, Eb etc. – calling out any words that come to mind to see if they trigger something in you, or in someone else for that matter.

In fact, in any situation where your team is struggling for an answer, people should keep lobbing out suggestions, however preposterous, because there's always a chance that something will click. For their part, team-mates to whom these thoughts are being pitched should keep an open mind as each arises, trying to look at it afresh. Just because the first three suggestions might be wide of the mark doesn't mean the fourth one will be.

Choose the 'percentage' alternative

If your team is torn between two answers, select the one you think most other teams are likely to go for, rather than the more exotic one. If you choose the popular answer and that turns out to be wrong, then only one or two teams are likely to gain a point at your expense. However, if you choose the more exotic answer and that turns out to be wrong, you'll lose a mark to most of the pub (and be in a bad mood for the rest of the quiz). Falling into this trap is rather like when footballers attempt the 'Hollywood' pass too often – great when it comes off, but it usually does more harm than good.

Complete the answer sheet carefully

Obvious as this may sound, it's easy to get carried away when you think of an answer and excitedly scribble something down that makes perfect sense to you but appears to resemble 'Toejam' or 'Snahdxrrv' to the person marking you.

Many people haven't owned a pencil since they were about twelve years old, but it's a good idea to use one when writing down answers to pub quizzes. Quite often the answer sheets allow little room in which to write the answer, and any mistake or subsequent change of mind can make things very messy if a pen is being used, whereas a pencil with an eraser solves that problem. And don't forget to bring a pencil sharpener and/or more than one pencil!

One golden rule is not to leave the answer blank if it doesn't immediately come to mind. Rather, jot down a pencilled note in that space to remind you of the question. If you don't do this, and you're struggling with three or four consecutive questions, your team's stress will be compounded if you can't remember which space to write in when you do eventually come up with an answer.

As a final check, get a team-mate to look over your shoulder as you write down the answer in case you've misheard what someone has said or have simply had a brainstorm (easily done if you're also trying to solve a sheet of word-searches and a bunch of anagrams at the same time).

Watch your spelling

It's best to try and spell your answers as accurately as you can, although most quizmasters will allow some leeway here. Things can get more complicated if one erroneous letter changes the sense of the word, or even the language, e.g. writing 'aqua' instead of 'agua' when asked the Spanish for water. Be very careful with chemical symbols to make sure you get your upper-and lower-case letters correct, otherwise you may suffer at the hands of fussy markers.

GAMESMANSHIP

In modern sport gamesmanship is a fact of life and pub quizzes are no different. I am not talking about out and out cheating here, which was covered in the previous chapter. Rather, I am describing methods which, although borderline, do not amount to flagrant cheating. A footballing parallel would be the tendency for every player to appeal for a throw-in even though they're fully aware that the ball went out off them.

Gamesmanship involves gaining a competitive advantage by dubious though legal means, and is therefore a necessary and appropriate weapon for your team to deploy if you are focused on winning your pub quiz. Look at it this way – your opponents will use these methods even if you don't, and your team doesn't want to be left behind. Let's look at some examples.

Fudging

If you can't quite recall whether the answer is the precise word you have in mind or something very similar, you may be able to 'fudge' it on the sheet in a way that keeps both options open. For example, if you're not certain whether to write Macau or Macaw, try writing down 'Maca', followed by an indistinct letter that could be taken to be a 'u' or a 'w' – maybe a 'u' with an extra bit of a tail!

Bet-hedging

In effect this involves writing down two (or even more) answers to the same question, but dressing this up in a very intelligent-looking way that may find favour with whoever is marking you. For example, in response to the question: 'What was Mother Teresa's nationality?' you might write down: 'Albanian*', and then at the bottom of the answer sheet add: '*She was born in Skopje in modern-day Macedonia, which was then part of the Ottoman Empire.'

NB: be aware that bet-hedging can engender one of two reactions on the part of the marking team:

1. an admiring comment written next to your novelette, to the effect of how brainy you are, accompanied by a smiley face; or

2. your sheet being returned to you in the form of a paper dart aimed at your head.

Fudging and Bet-hedging

1. *Macau*

Fudging, to cover yourself if you are uncertain whether to write Macau or Macaw

2. ....

3. *Albanian* *

Hedging your bets, where you think there might be more than one possible answer to the question of Mother Teresa's nationality.

4. ....

* But she was born in Skopje in modern Macadonia which was part of the Ottoman Empire at the time.

Overhearing answers

As noted earlier, it is very handy when a nearby team blurts out the answer within your earshot, so it may work to your advantage to choose a table next to a noisy but capable team in order to maximise this possibility. In the case of multi-choice questions, keep an eye out for those talented but demonstrative teams who tend to indulge in a bout of exaggerated head-nodding or shaking as each option is read out.

Benign reciprocity

If answer sheets are to be swapped for marking by another team rather than by the quizmaster, choose a team which appears to be (a) not very good and (b) extremely friendly, then mark their papers generously, highlighting that you have done so (this works best if marking is done on a round-by-round basis so they can see from the start how kind you're being). They will not come close to beating you but you may expect to benefit from some equally benign marking (cynical I know, but we're not here to make up the numbers). Here's an example:

1. London   1

2. Rhine   0

3. Swaziland ½ – Marking a poor team generously
(in this case the required answer was Switzerland!)

4. Everest   0

5. Antarctica 0

Total for round: 1½

TEAM ROLES

Individual players tend to adopt one or more roles within their teams. Some of these are useful, others less so, but it's important to be aware of what they are, and how best to exploit them to the advantage of the team, as follows:

Leader: the purpose of this role is to make a ruling if the team is split on possible answers, to allocate sheets to players in the event of multiple handout rounds, and to make other key decisions, e.g. whether to raise an objection with the quizmaster.

Facilitator: this person's job is to ensure that everyone's voice is heard. It is an optional role but becomes useful if the leader is a fascist.

Quizmaster liaison: this role's only task is to raise any points of contention with the quizmaster, with the aim of blagging more points for the team, e.g. 'I know the answer is that trains for Hogwarts leave King's Cross from Platform 9¾ but we put 9½ – surely you can allow us a quarter of a platform either side?' The pre-requisites for this role are long hair, bedroom eyes and a seriously short skirt (NB, this look tends to work best if you're female).

Official Scribe: the one who writes down the team's answers – must be literate, neat and adept at fudging (see above).

Answer Scribe: this person copies down your team's answers and is thus able to tally your score for instant comparison with your marked sheet when it's handed back to you, allowing discrepancies to be immediately highlighted.

Marker: the person on your team who marks the neighbouring team's answer sheet – must be fair-minded but firm, and alert to opportunities for benign reciprocity (see above).

Now here are a few other roles which, though common, may not be so helpful:

Naysayer (loud): spends the whole quiz reacting to every suggestion by a team-mate with: 'I don't know what the answer is but I'm pretty sure it's not THAT.'

Naysayer (quiet): utters no more than one thing during the entire quiz (maybe: 'It's definitely not Bet Lynch') but then bursts into life as the answers are read out, saying on multiple occasions: 'Do you know what, I THOUGHT it might be him,' which in turn attracts exasperated cries of: 'Well, why the bloody hell didn't you say so?'

The Ego: this person insists their suggestions are always right and will brook no argument to the contrary. When it turns out they are wrong, they totally face down their team-mates, unapologetically and without the merest hint of embarrassment.

Quiz rage maniac: urbane, intelligent and usually charming guy who becomes bizarrely psychotic when he disagrees with the quizmaster's adjudication.

Stage whisperer: says things like: 'Do you really think the answer is Schopenhauer?' at 128 decibels, and within earshot of seven rival teams who until that point did not have a clue.

TEAM ETIQUETTE

Behaving well at pub quizzes is not just the decent thing to do. It can also work in your team's favour when you do eventually become serial winners, because it gives opponents less reason to hate you, and hence mark you severely. Here are five examples of the sort of people who do not 'get' pub quiz etiquette:

1. Anyone who doesn't put their mobile phone away. Even if it's switched off, just having the thing visible is sufficient provocation to make certain types of opposing player want to come over to the owner's table and disembowel them.

2. Teams that start up a loud conversation when they've got the answer while other teams are still struggling – it's not big and it's not clever.

3. Teams who start up a loud conversation just as the quizmaster is reading the question and then bellow, 'Didn't catch that!' as if it were somehow his fault that they haven't heard it.

4. Teams that mark harshly – better to mark other teams generously (unless they contain a man called Norman) with the aim of benefiting from some benign reciprocity.

5. People who get ratty when they lose. Or say: 'If we hadn't talked ourselves out of those six answers, we would have won,' because the chances are that the winning team (and every other team in the pub for that matter) will have also talked themselves out of six answers.

Now, of course, by the time you finish this book, Rule 5 will have become irrelevant because your team will have grown into an all-conquering juggernaut, but don't forget that winning too has its own etiquette. So for starters, remember not to clap yourselves when your team is announced as the winners – in fact, don't move a single muscle in your body other than those facial ones that generate your most appealing 'Aw shucks' expression.

Being announced as the winner of the pub quiz can be a quite wonderful sensation, not least because the process of milking the plaudits can, if you are lucky, extend across no less than four distinct phases: (1) the initial burst of applause when the results are announced, (2) the generous words of praise from the quizmaster that may follow after the clapping dies down (more applause), (3) the award of the cash prize, vinegar or de-rusting agent (more applause), and (4) the final congratulations from vanquished opponents as they troop out of the pub.

Before I started to win a few quizzes, I used to observe how victorious teams responded to plaudits, and I gradually came to appreciate what they were doing. I have now formalised this into my Magnanimous Victory Acknowledgement Decoder©, which goes like this: To the compliment: 'Well played – you deserved to win tonight', here is what winning teams tend to say, followed by what they actually mean:

What they say

- We were lucky. The questions just fell right for us tonight.

- We just enjoyed a good day at the office.

- We were amazed when he read out the scores – we thought we'd blown it on the Film Round.

What they mean

- Of course we deserved to win. And we found it dead easy too – just like we always do.

- Every day at the office is a good day for us. You'll never be smart enough to work in our office, matey.

- We weren't really amazed. We just needed something nice to say in case we were congratulated by losers like you.

PUB NAMES

Royalty is a major source of pub names hence The Crown, The King's Head and, of course, The Queen Vic. The Royal Oak commemorates the escape of the future King Charles II at the Battle of Worcester by hiding in an oak tree.

Pubs located near royal hunting grounds assumed related names such as The Hare and Hounds, The Fox and Hounds or The Dog and Duck.

Pubs named The Bull, The Bear or The Cock may well derive from the pastimes of the day – bull or bear baiting, and cock-fighting.

The word 'arms' in a pub name refers to coats of arms – the heraldic symbols adopted by knights to distinguish them in battle.

The White Hart is an heraldic device, being mainly associated with the reign of Richard II.

The Red Lion has been associated with two men of immense power in their day – John of Gaunt, who established the reign of the House of Lancaster, and King James I.

During a time of massive pub expansion in the eighteenth and early nineteenth centuries, many pubs were named after military and naval heroes such as The Duke of Wellington and The Admiral Nelson.

NOW TEST YOURSELF

MEDIUM

1. Who managed Portsmouth to their FA Cup victory in 2008?

2. Which country was known to the Romans as Cambria?

3. What is the Italian name for Turin?

4. Which 1970s hit begins with the words: 'Oh, it's been a long long time, looks like I got you off my mind'?

5. What is the connection between the above answers?

(Answers on page 127)

So, that is all you need to know in order to turn your pub quiz team into a winning machine. However, this will only work if your team is made up of competent quizzers, so we are now set to embark on a series of chapters designed to improve your personal quizzing ability. But first, I need to perform another of my quiz fact drills, and this time it's shipbuilding during the twentieth century – should be riveting.

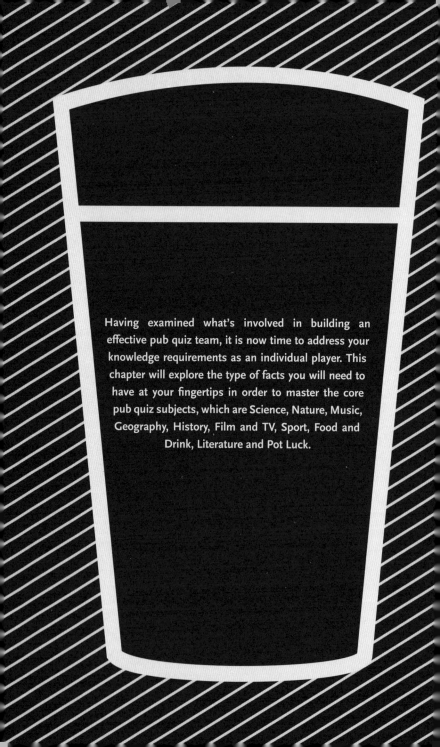

Having examined what's involved in building an effective pub quiz team, it is now time to address your knowledge requirements as an individual player. This chapter will explore the type of facts you will need to have at your fingertips in order to master the core pub quiz subjects, which are Science, Nature, Music, Geography, History, Film and TV, Sport, Food and Drink, Literature and Pot Luck.

4

KNOW MORE HEROES

**UNDERSTANDING
PUB QUIZ FACTS**

Pub Quiz Trivia vs Real Knowledge

Let's start with an example from the Geography round, namely the country of Albania. A non-quizzer faced with the task of learning about Albania might choose to examine its population and ethnic make-up, its language and culture, the physical geography and major cities, its history under the Ottoman Empire and since, and its current political and social structure. If asked to present that information, they might write a lengthy essay or prepare a 30-slide Powerpoint pack. An experienced quizzer, on the other hand, will drill straight into a specific set of key pub quiz facts:

- Capital – Tirana

- Nickname – Land of the Eagles

- Flag – black double-headed eagle on red background

- Currency – Lek

- Last King – Zog (pre-WW2)

- First socialist leader – Enver Hoxha (post-WW2)

- Favourite comedian – Norman Wisdom

- Throne once offered to – C.B. Fry

- Most famous Albanian – Mother Teresa

Sorry, Albania, but that's about it – I'm afraid there really isn't much else to say. But the good news for the reader is that, from a quizzing perspective, an entire country can be mastered in about two minutes. So, when confronted by a new topic, how can you acquire the 'nose' to sniff out what's going to help you win the quiz without making it a lifetime's study? One way of looking at the world of quiz knowledge is to break it down into three layers: the General Knowledge Layer, the List Layer and the Trivia Layer. Let's illustrate this by taking snooker as an example:

1. General Knowledge Layer – the basic rules, the terminology and the names and nicknames of the more well-known players e.g. Ali (The Captain) Carter

2. List Layer – the winners of the Snooker World Championship from 1970 to the present day

3. Trivia Layer – for example, that Ronnie (The Rocket) O'Sullivan's middle name is Antonio or that it was The Matchroom Mob with Chas & Dave who released that irritating 1986 hit 'Snooker Loopy'

What you wouldn't need to know is anything about the major overseas tournaments – quizmasters take a pretty UK-centric view so that doesn't tend to get asked. Nor would you need to worry about how the game developed – no doubt an interesting read but a barren source of pub quiz questions.

Let's now take a journey through the major quiz-round categories, using the Three Layer Model to highlight the sort of facts you will need to become a proficient pub quizzer.

Science

General Knowledge Layer

Science is a good place to start because I've never understood the first thing about it yet I'd still expect to score seven or eight out of ten in any reasonable Science round. Science involves a lot of analysis and measurement, so let's take something called the Mohs scale as an example of what I'm saying.

The Mohs scale has nothing to do with the barman in *The Simpsons*. Rather, it is used to measure the **hardness** of a substance, running from **one = talc** to **ten = diamond** (which is so hard that the hardest diamonds can only be scratched by other diamonds). I'm OK at the diamond end of the scale, but why talc, for goodness' sake? Surely there must be things that are softer than talc – what about jelly or slugs? And if diamond is worth ten, what about Roy Keane and Vinnie Jones? A nine at least, I would have thought. Either way, it's not a problem if you don't actually understand the Mohs Scale – all that matters are the three bold facts.

If you whizz through a few halfway decent Physics or Chemistry rounds in any quizbook, you'll quickly find that the Mohs Scale is one of relatively few quiz-friendly topics at the General Knowledge level, because most science is too complex and stodgy to break down into pub quiz questions. Therefore, the basics of science from a quizzing perspective can easily be learned.

List Layer

The Periodic Table is the most obvious example of a Science list. Some people find memorising any of this pretty tough, while others are in their, ahem, element. But either way, there's no need to learn all the chemical symbols – about 20 to 30 of the more common ones should suffice. Similarly, you shouldn't worry about all the atomic numbers, perhaps confining yourself to the first ten, then 50 (Tin) and 100 (Fermium) and maybe Silver (47) and Gold (79), which could be useful in a tie-break. And then perhaps a few key facts about some of the better-known elements (Hydrogen was discovered by Sir Henry Cavendish, Mercury is also known as hydrargyrum (from the Greek for water and silver), hence its chemical symbol Hg, and Aluminium is the most abundant metal in the Earth's crust).

SI Units are another good example of a learnable list. If you get to know about ten of these you should be Ohm and dry, provided your Lux in.

Trivia Layer

Although Albert Einstein was a world-famous historical figure who formulated the Theory of Relativity ($e=mc^2$) and was subsequently awarded the Nobel Prize for Physics in 1921, he is best known in pub quiz circles for never wearing socks.

Going back to diamonds, it's worth knowing that they are measured by the 'Four Cs' – clarity, carat, cut and colour – and that a perfect diamond is known as a paragon. More importantly, however, Diamond was also the name of Sir Isaac Newton's dog who, according to legend, knocked over a lighted candle in his study, thus destroying years of documented research.

10 KEY FACTS
OXYGEN

1. Chemical symbol = O; atomic number = 8
2. Joseph Priestley is generally credited with its discovery in 1774*
3. O_2 (aka Dioxygen) is Oxygen's most stable form
4. Air contains approximately 21 per cent Oxygen
5. Oxygen is the most abundant element by mass in the Earth's Crust
6. It is also the most abundant element by mass in the human body
7. It is the third most abundant element in the universe (after Hydrogen and Helium)
8. The ozone (O_3) layer is in the stratosphere
9. The phrase 'the oxygen of publicity' was coined by Margaret Thatcher
10. 'Love Is Like Oxygen' was a No. 9 hit for The Sweet in January 1978.

*Swedish scientist Carl Wilhelm Scheele is believed to have discovered Oxygen a couple of years earlier but did not publish his findings until after Priestley.

Nature

General Knowledge Layer

For pub quiz purposes, Nature breaks down into Botany, Zoology and Human Biology. General botanical knowledge such as the respiratory or reproductive systems of plants is not an easily digestible subject so many questions at this level tend to cover more mundane topics such as fruit varieties, e.g. mayduke is a type of cherry (as are merton glory, morello, montmorency and maraschino – basically, if it begins with M and you're not sure, go for cherry).

Zoology offers a far wider range of facts at the general knowledge level with multiple questions about extreme animals: e.g. largest fish = whale shark, smallest bird = bee hummingbird, fastest animal = cheetah. Also, fish that do tricks tend to crop up frequently, such as the Archer Fish – fells insects by spitting water at them; Fighting Fish – builds nests out of bubbles; and Puffer Fish – can inflate themselves into spiny balls.

Human Biology is also a bounteous source of quiz questions, often involving numbers (206 bones, 24 ribs, 32 teeth) and alternative names – bronchitis is the 'English Disease' while syphilis is the 'French Disease' (although the latter term could be extended to being crap at winning wars and intra-squad squabbling at major football tournaments). Talking of which, Hansen's Disease is another term for leprosy and not, as you might have imagined, smug TV soccer punditry.

List Layer

Alternative names are well worth knowing in the field of Botany and there are hundreds of them for plants (e.g. tradescantia = wandering Jew), fruit (e.g. avocado = alligator pear) and trees (e.g. araucaria = Chile pine = monkey puzzle tree).

Collective nouns for animals are another pub quiz staple, such as an ambush of tigers, an intrusion of cockroaches and a troubling (why?) of goldfish. Of course, these continue to evolve and I'd like to share a couple of more recent ones – an obsession of pub quizzers and a fussiness of quizmasters.

Trivia Layer

In Zoology numbers really come into their own, revealing some truly bizarre facts, for example that ants have five noses, octopuses have three hearts and caterpillars have twelve eyes. Dog facts are proliferating with the popularity of rare breeds, and also cross-breeds such as labradoodles (annoyingly, the dog-naming police have settled upon the term 'shih-poo' to describe a cross between a shih tzu and a poodle – I think they may have missed a trick there). And in the field of Human Biology, Louise Brown became the first test-tube baby in 1978 under the pioneering regime of Patrick Steptoe (he'd sent Harold out to do the round that day).

Music

General Knowledge Layer

Music is a wide-ranging and fast-changing field of knowledge. The staple fare of pop music is song titles and artists, which can throw up some rather weird juxtapositions. For example, those unnatural bedfellows Russ Abbott and Joy Division both had hits with songs called 'Atmosphere' in the 1980s, and in similar vein both Bruce Springsteen and Ken Dodd have enjoyed Top 40 success with singles entitled 'The River'.

Lyrics questions are also extremely popular and these can get quite convoluted, for example: In 'Up the Junction' by Squeeze, at what time did the girl from Clapham have the baby? Answer: 5.20 a.m. ('This morning at 4:50, I took her rather nifty down to an incubator where 30 minutes later she gave birth to a daughter ...').

Of course the names of band members crop up regularly. If you're struggling to name the lead vocalist in any indie band of the last ten years, just answer 'Tom' and you may get half a point, subject to the quizmaster's generosity. If you then add 'Smith' to cover all bases, you would actually earn the full point if the band in question was Editors.

List Layer

Once again, the 'list list' is huge, including:

- **No. 1s by year** – well over a thousand of these now since the charts started in 1952, and trending upwards (in 1984 there were just 13 No. 1s, whereas in 2011 there were 33 of them)

- **Christmas No. 1s** (if in doubt think of your least favourite record from the year in question and that will be it)

- Real names of pop artists (e.g. Gary Numan = Gary Webb, Cliff Richard = Harry Webb)

- **Former names of bands** (for example, Creedence Clearwater Revival were once known as The Golliwogs – why ever did they change it?)

Trivia Layer

Here are some tricky questions:

🍺 **'The lyrics of which 1970s No. 1 hit contains the title of the single that replaced it at No. 1?'**

The answer is 'Bohemian Rhapsody' by Queen, which contains the words 'Mamma Mia' (Abba) – about 2 hours and 18 minutes into the track, it's the bit that Freddie sings like he's got a clothes peg clipped to his nose.

🍺 **'What is Paul McCartney's middle name?'**

The answer, I'm afraid, is Paul (his full name is James Paul McCartney). Bad quizmaster, naughty quizmaster.

🍺 **'How old was 1960s star Heinz when he died?'**

To which your initial reaction might be: 'How the hell should I know?' But in a decent quiz there is always a purpose to seemingly impossible questions, and the answer is 57 (think baked beans).

In summary, with the Music round above all others there are no easy routes to proficiency, apart from trying to ensure that your team spans every era, and ideally includes coverage of classical music and songs from the shows.

Geography

General Knowledge Layer

Some of the most common types of question within this category involve longest rivers, biggest lakes, highest mountains etc., both worldwide and within each continent. For example, Mount Everest is the highest mountain in the world, followed by K2 (aka Godwin-Austen), and then Kanchenjunga, all of which are in the Himalayas.

Next you'll need to master some basic facts about most countries (e.g. Albania – see above), as well as the world's major cities (e.g. Florence – key facts to which are Tuscany, Arno, Uffizi, Ponte Vecchio and the annual influx of Brits called Benedict and Jemima).

Remember also that Geology falls into this category – for example, the three types of rock are igneous, metamorphic and sedimentary (my dear Watson).

List Layer

The obvious examples here are:

- Capital cities – unfortunately there are over 200 of them, and for every Paris there is a Ngerulmud (Palau).

- US state capitals and their nicknames (for every Texas/Austin/Lone Star State there is a North Dakota/Bismarck/Peace Garden State)

- Flags – best to learn about 50 of the most well-known countries, plus Nepal (the world's only national non-rectangular flag)

- Currencies – this time about a hundred should do, which is not as hard as it sounds because common denominations such as Euro, Dollar, Pound, Franc, Dinar and Peso are shared by several nations (as a general rule, if you don't know the answer and the country in question is down at heel, put 'Euro').

And somewhat less obviously:

- Sea Areas (about which most people know Rockall)

- International dialling codes (generally, those starting with 1 = North America, 2 = Africa, 3 & 4 = Europe, 5 = Latin America, 6 = Oceania & South East Asia, 7 = former Soviet Union, and 8 & 9 = Asia).

- International car registration codes – it's best to start with the single-letter countries (A for Austria, B for Belgium etc.), though some people think that any quizmaster who throws in this type of question is a bit of a Germany, Italy, Cuba, Cambodia.

Trivia Layer

None, because Geography teachers do not possess a sense of humour.

History

General Knowledge Layer

A classic question of this type is: 'Who was murdered in Sarajevo on 28 June 1914?' and of course the answer is Archduke Franz Ferdinand of Austria, whose assassination by Gavrilo Princip led directly to the outbreak of World War I.

Dates feature heavily, naturally, for example: 'In which year was the Battle of Stamford Bridge?' The answer is 1066, one month before the Battle of Hastings, when King Harold had to march his army up to Yorkshire to see off the allied forces of his own brother Tostig and Norwegian King Harald Hardrada (Harold's victory owed much to a massed defensive manoeuvre known as 'parking the bus', which has been successfully deployed on a number of subsequent occasions at that venue).

List Layer

History is full of lists, e.g. Kings and Queens, Prime Ministers and US Presidents. As well as the relevant dates, it's useful to log a key fact or two, such as their greatest achievements e.g. Winston Churchill (victory in World War Two), Clement Attlee (National Health Service) and John Major (Cones Hotline).

Nicknames are also useful for quiz purposes, as in the case of US Presidents. For example, Ronald Reagan was known both as 'Dutch' and 'The Great Communicator', while Abraham Lincoln's nicknames included 'The Great Emancipator'. Calvin Coolidge was known as 'Silent Cal' because of his pithy style, as evidenced by a possibly apocryphal conversation with Dorothy Parker who, seated next to him at a dinner, said: 'Mr Coolidge, I've made a bet against a fellow who said it was impossible to get more than two words out of you,' to which he is supposed to have shot back: 'You lose.'

Trivia Layer

Horses and quotes are the key to historical trivia. Famous horses in History include Copenhagen (Wellington), Marengo (Napoleon), Bucephalus (Alexander the Great), Incitatus (Caligula) and Toytown (Zara Phillips).

Winston Churchill is an excellent source of quotes, not least those directed against his Labour adversary Clement Attlee. On one occasion when they bumped into each other in the House of Commons toilets, Attlee asked Churchill why he appeared to have chosen a urinal as far away from him as possible, to which Churchill replied: 'I have no quarrel with you, but in my experience, when you see something that's big and works well, you tend to want to nationalise it.'

Film and TV

General Knowledge Layer

Film and TV is an immensely varied and expanding subject in which the minimum requirement for any team is to know the main actors in the more popular UK and US movies and TV programmes, past and present. As regards films, this means going back to the advent of talkies in the late 1920s, including some of the main directors. In the case of TV, you are looking at major series since the 1950s, including character names (and in long-running soaps like *Coronation Street* and *EastEnders* this can be pretty daunting).

10 KEY FACTS
CLARK GABLE

1. William Clark Gable, 1901–60
2. Nickname: 'King of Hollywood'
3. Won Best Actor Oscar for *It Happened One Night*, 1934
4. Nominated in 1935 for *Mutiny On The Bounty* (playing Fletcher Christian)
5. Nominated 1939 for *Gone With The Wind* (playing Rhett Butler)
6. Most famous line: 'Frankly, my dear, I don't give a damn'
7. Married Carole Lombard, who died in a plane crash in 1942
8. Favourite actor of Hitler, who offered a reward for his capture
9. WW2 discharge papers signed by Captain Ronald Reagan (yes, him!)
10. Final film – *The Misfits* (released 1961, which was also Marilyn Monroe's last completed film).

List Layer

It's vital to know your Oscar winners and years, plus a few key facts about them. For example, Katharine Hepburn has won the most Best Actor/ Actress awards (four), though she was not always highly regarded, having been branded 'box office poison' during the 1930s when Dorothy Parker (again!) said of one performance: 'Katharine Hepburn runs the gamut of emotions from A to B.'

James Bond films are another list-friendly area (titles, lead actors, villains, 'girls', and theme songs and singers), plus related facts, for example that Sean Connery's middle name is Sean (his full name is Thomas Sean Connery) and that Roger Moore was 45 at the time of his Bond debut in *Live and Let Die*.

In the case of TV, the actors who have played Doctor Who now constitute a sizeable list (including two Bakers: Tom – 4th and Colin – 6th), as do the winners of the myriad reality shows which, for convenience, may be summarised as *Big Brother's Celebrity Apprentice Bake-Off on Ice* (a sizeable Z-List, in that case).

Trivia Layer

This layer runs very deep in both TV and film. Most famous films have their accompanying trivia, for example the bus mustn't drop below 50mph in *Speed*, while in *Back to the Future* the DeLorean has to reach 88mph to exit the present day. Film taglines occur frequently, e.g. 'A tale of murder, lust, greed, revenge, and seafood' (*A Fish Called Wanda*), as do quotes, e.g. 'You talkin' to me?' (Travis Bickle, played by Robert de Niro in *Taxi Driver*) or the oft-imitated 'You're only supposed to blow the bloody doors off' (Michael Caine as Charlie Croker in *The Italian Job*).

In TV many of the classic comedy series carry a range of attendant trivia – for example, Manuel's rat in *Fawlty Towers* was called Basil, while the cockerel in *The Good Life* was called Lenin. *Gavin and Stacey* attracted controversy because the surnames of the families were those of mass murderers – Shipman and West. Addresses also make frequent appearances in quizzes, for example 368 Nelson Mandela House (*Only Fools and Horses*), 112½ Beacon Street (*Cheers*) and 742 Evergreen Terrace (*The Simpsons*).

And we couldn't leave this section without mentioning the pub quiz trivia classic that the first couple to be shown in bed together on prime-time

TV were Fred and Wilma Flintstone (though in the USA this honour in fact belongs to Mary Kay and Johnny, co stars of a sitcom of that name from the late 1940s).

Overall, the key to quiz success in Film and TV is to be able to divvy this lot up around a balanced team – maybe a film buff and two or three TV fans of different generations.

Sport

General Knowledge Layer

In addition to developing a detailed knowledge of the more popular sports such as football, tennis and golf, it's important to learn a few basic facts about some of the more obscure sports. For example:

- the areas of snooker, table tennis and pool tables (in feet) are 12x6, 9x5 and 7x4 respectively

- the original name for lacrosse was bagattaway, while that of badminton was poona

- basketball was invented by James Naismith and volleyball by William G. Morgan

Sports stars' nicknames crop up regularly in quizzes, well-known examples being 'Guy the Gorilla' (Ian Botham), 'The Dark Destroyer' (Nigel Benn) and 'The Great White Shark' (Greg 'I owe a lot to my parents, especially my mother and father' Norman).

List Layer

Sport is list heaven. Football is full of lists, for example League Champions, FA Cup winners, and World Cup winners and host countries. Football ground questions also occur frequently, e.g. Stoke City, who in 1997 moved from the Victoria Ground to the Britannia Stadium (where Sir Stanley Matthews' ashes are buried beneath the centre circle).

Cricket and rugby World Cup winners and host countries also feature prominently as well as their key events, e.g. the bone-crunching debut of

Western Samoa in the 1991 tournament in which they battered Wales to defeat at Cardiff Arms Park, leading one Welsh wag to remark: 'Thank God we weren't playing all of Samoa!'

Other major lists include Wimbledon and Open Golf Champions, as well as Olympic venues and major performers. And, of course, winners of the BBC Sports Personality of the Year award (only Henry Cooper, Nigel Mansell and Damon Hill have won it more than once, while Hill and his father Graham, and Zara Phillips and the Princess Royal, are the only offspring/parent winners).

Trivia Layer

Here are some typical sporting trivia questions:

'In the world of sport, what links a New York borough, a Shakespeare character, a Spanish cross and a Canadian Prime Minister?'
The answer is that they are the first names of David Beckham's children – Brooklyn, Romeo, Cruz and Harper.

'About whom did Liverpool fans chant: "He's big, he's red, his feet stick out the bed" between 2005 and 2008?'
Answer: Peter Crouch who, when asked what he would have been had he not become a footballer, memorably replied: 'A virgin!'

'Which cricketer acquired the nickname "King of Spain" in 2000?'
The answer is Ashley Giles, who was England's leading spinner in the 2005 Ashes-winning team (a set of mugs ordered during his testimonial year in 2000 were erroneously printed with that slogan, instead of 'King of Spin'!)

Food and Drink

General Knowledge Layer

Most Food and Drink facts involve the names of dishes and their main ingredients, and these can be learned quite easily without needing any culinary expertise whatsoever. For example, it is a constant source of irritation to my wife, who is an excellent cook, that it was I and not she who was able to answer the question: 'Which fruit is encased in a Sussex Pond Pudding?' The answer is a (whole) lemon and it doesn't matter if you don't know how to make a Sussex Pond Pudding nor even if you've never tasted one – you simply need to know about the lemon.

Other commonly asked Food and Drink questions involve wine and their country or region of origin, linked dishes such as Angels on Horseback (oysters wrapped in bacon) and Devils on Horseback (prunes wrapped in bacon), and misnomers such as Glamorgan Sausage (which is largely composed of cheese) and Bombay Duck (which is a type of fish).

List Layer

The Drink part of the topic contains the most lists, for example beer-barrel sizes and the biblical names for outsize wine bottles, and it would pay to learn about 30 of the better-known cocktails and their ingredients (Sex on the Beach, anyone?). Perhaps the main food list is that of cheeses and their animal and country of origin (you'll need to tread Caerphilly there).

Trivia Layer

Food and Drink offers quite a rich source (or should that be sauce?) of quiz fact trivia. For example:

- George Bush at a press conference in 1990 announced that he had a lifelong dislike of broccoli

- Horseradish was the first product to be promoted under the Heinz company's '57 Varieties' advertising campaign

- Yarg is a Cornish cheese that takes its name from the Gray family, who provided the recipe to the modern producers (reverse the letters)

- A Berliner is a type of German doughnut – it is often reported that President Kennedy, when giving a speech in Berlin in 1963, stated that he was a doughnut because he used the phrase '*Ich bin ein Berliner*' rather than saying '*Ich bin Berliner*' (though there is a argument to the effect that his inclusion of '*ein*' was a valid means of associating himself with the people of Berlin without saying that he was literally from Berlin).

Cross-linkage to other categories such as Film provides a further set of Food and Drink trivia, for example:

- Gangsters Jules and Vincent enjoyed an extensive discussion about a burger known as a Royale with Cheese while en route to an assignment in *Pulp Fiction*.

- Paul Newman's character in *Cool Hand Luke* ate 50 hard-boiled eggs in an hour for a bet.

- Hannibal Lecter reminisced about a meal of human liver and fava beans with a nice Chianti in *The Silence of the Lambs*.

Finally, we should not forget TV chefs. For example, famous as Delia Smith has become during the last 30 years, she probably baked her most enduring creation as early as 1969 in the form of a cake that featured in the artwork for the cover of the Rolling Stones' *Let It Bleed* album.

Top 10 Quiz Dishes

1. Nerd's Nest Soup
2. Quizzotto
3. Dork Scratchings
4. Haute Quizine
5. Lemon Nerd Tart
6. Thai-break Chicken
7. Quizcotti
8. Cheaton Mess
9. Geek Salad
10. Belly of Dork

Literature

General Knowledge Layer

The most commonly asked questions in this category concern the names of the authors, playwrights or poets behind the more well-known works of literature. The number of titles required for quizzing purposes amounts to over a thousand, the only consolation being that this is not expanding at the rate of pop singles or films.

Where the writer or a particular work is especially well known, such as Shakespeare, Sherlock Holmes or the Harry Potter series, then a slightly deeper level of knowledge will be needed. Agatha Christie (1890–1976) provides a good example. She was born Agatha Miller and wrote romances under the name of Mary Westmacott, but her most famous creations are Miss (Jane) Marple and Hercule Poirot, the Belgian detective who was supported by his friend, Captain Arthur Hastings and his secretary, Miss Felicity Lemon. Christie is also remembered for disappearing for eleven days in 1926, and for her play *The Mousetrap*, which remains the longest-running production on the London stage, having opened in 1952.

List Layer

The titles of all the Shakespeare plays and Dickens novels need to be memorised along with their main characters and storylines. Also, it's important to know the names behind the initials that a lot of authors have tended to adopt, for example Dorothy L(eigh) Sayers, A(lan) A(lexander) Milne and A(ntonia) S(usan) Byatt (who is the sister of Margaret Drabble).

Trivia Layer

Literature is rich in trivia, for example:

- Shakespeare's son was called Hamnet while AA Milne's was called Christopher Robin

- The words 'Elementary, my dear Watson' did not feature in any of the Sherlock Holmes' books, only in subsequent film adaptations etc.

- Robert Louis Stephenson is commonly believed, at least for pub quiz purposes, to have died while making mayonnaise

- Anthony Trollope invented the pillar box

Quotes by literary figures feature prominently in pub quizzes, and if you don't know the answer you'd be well advised to guess either Mark Twain if you think the author might be American, or Oscar Wilde if the quote sounds more British in style. Among Twain's most well-known quotes are 'When in doubt tell the truth', 'The reports of my death are greatly exaggerated', and the ahead-of-its-time and really quite zany 'A cauliflower is nothing but a cabbage with a college education'.

Wilde's classics include 'I can resist everything except temptation', 'Work is the curse of the drinking classes' as well as 'Bigamy is having one wife too many; monogamy is the same' (though the source of that quote is not proven despite it usually being attributed to Wilde).

Pot Luck

General Knowledge Layer

Pot Luck is basically everything that hasn't been covered so far, so this will range from discrete, chunky topics like Religion or Mythology through to the cornucopia of miscellany that quizmasters love to throw in, such as questions about the signs of the zodiac, gemstones and wedding anniversaries. Beware getting caught out by regularly updated facts such as the price of a first-class stamp or the current weekly minimum wage (they're approximately the same these days). Folksy knowledge also comes into this category, such as proverbs and nursery rhymes.

Word definitions are another regular occurrence under Pot Luck, for example Triskaidekaphobia is a fear of the number 13, autophobia is the fear of loneliness (not an affliction that troubles many pub quizzers, fortunately), while nomophobia (genuinely, apparently) is the fear of having no mobile phone contact, which is of course common among pub quiz cheats.

List Layer

The Pot Luck category is characterised by long lists of miscellany. For example, Bingo Lingo betrays a somewhat misogynistic bent, with 88 represented by the expression 'Two Fat Ladies', 30 by 'Dirty Gertie' and 76 by 'Was she worth it?' (7/6d being the price of a marriage licence back in the day – maybe the modern equivalent might be 'forty three, civil ceremon-ee'). Other lists include the ancient gods and goddesses (Juno many?), books of the Bible (not that old Malachi) and archaic terms for weights and measures (which some find hard to fathom). And we shouldn't forget cockney rhyming slang, both traditional – Adam and Eve = believe and Mince Pies = eyes – or more recent such as Barack Obama = llama and Osama Bin Laden = garden (as in 'I cannot Adam and Eve my mince pies; I've just seen a Barack in the Osama').

Trivia Layer

You may have thought that every fact so far mentioned under Pot Luck has been pretty trivial, but let's finish with a few pieces of übertrivia:

- Swindon Town is the only league football club whose name does not contain any of the letters in the word 'mackerel'

- The surnames of Barbie and Ken are Roberts and Carson respectively.

- HB in pencil hardness measurement stands for 'Hard Black', while WNA on the Plimsoll Line stands for 'Winter North Atlantic'

- The black box on an aeroplane is orange

- The Greek national anthem has 158 verses

- Roulette is known as 'The Devil's Game' because the numbers on the wheel add up to 666.

- St John's Wood is the only London Underground station whose name does not contain any of the letters in the word 'mackerel'

RANDOM PUB FACTS

- There are approximately 50,000 pubs in the UK.

- The British pub industry employs around 600,000 people.

- Over 15 million people drink in pubs every week.

- UK pubs serve over a billion meals per year.

- The most popular pub names in the UK are The Red Lion and The Crown.

- The largest pub in the UK is the Regal in Cambridge, previously a cinema which was built in 1937 and seated 1,300 people.

- The smallest pub in the UK is the Signal Box in Cleethorpes though The Nutshell in Bury St Edmunds is currently the official smallest pub in the Guinness World Records.

- The lowest pub in England is the Admiral Wells in Peterborough which is 2.7m (9ft) below sea level.

- The highest pub is the Tan Inn in the Yorkshire Dales, which is 518m (1,700ft) above sea level.

- The pub with the longest name in the UK is The Old Thirteenth Cheshire Astley Volunteer Rifleman Corps Inn, located in Stalybridge, Greater Manchester.

TOUGHER

1. Which soil-tilling machine was patented in 1920 by Arthur Clifford Howard in New South Wales?

2. In music what comes between a crotchet and a semibreve?

3. There are two types of canoeing events in the Olympics – one is the Canadian; name the other.

4. Sir Robert Alexander Watson-Watt is considered by many to have been the inventor of what in the mid-1930s?

5. What is the connection between the above answers?

(Answers on page 127)

And on that note of high erudition, our journey through the world of quiz facts fizzles to a halt. Before proceeding to the next stage in our self-improvement programme, I need to tackle another of my quiz fact drills. This time it's Hampshire Rivers – should be quite a Test.

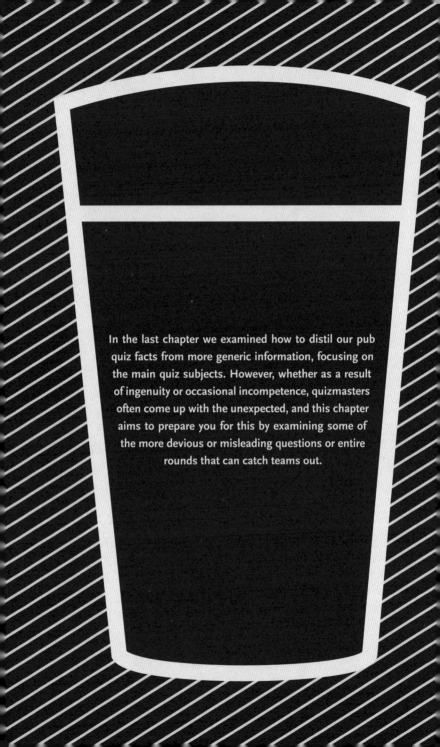

In the last chapter we examined how to distil our pub quiz facts from more generic information, focusing on the main quiz subjects. However, whether as a result of ingenuity or occasional incompetence, quizmasters often come up with the unexpected, and this chapter aims to prepare you for this by examining some of the more devious or misleading questions or entire rounds that can catch teams out.

A QUIZTION OF TASTE

**TIPS FOR TRICKY QUESTIONS
AND ROUNDS**

TIPS FOR TRICKY QUESTIONS

Anagrams

To get things started, here is an anagram:

THAT GREAT CHARMER (clue – famous 20th-century figure – 8,8)

Anagrams usually come with a clue, plus an indication of the letter count per word, and there is a classic three-step technique for solving them, as follows:

Step 1: on a separate sheet, redraw the letters into a circle – this helps to highlight different sequences and combinations of letters.

Step 2: focus on any of the rarer letters (the high Scrabble scorers) such as K, J, X, Q and Z to see if they suggest an obvious and possibly significant word.

Step 3: look out for commonly occurring letter combinations such as 'ing' or 'ness' to draw out one or more of the key words.

That is the standard approach to solving anagrams (the answer above is Margaret Thatcher in case you hadn't sussed it).

Here's another one to test whether you've grasped the concept: **AHA, REG – MANTRAS** (your clue is people who hate anagrams – 7,6). Speaking as one such anagram hater, I tend to favour an alternative approach:

Step 1: complete Steps 1 to 3 above in eight seconds.

Step 2: utter a short expletive such as **SLOB LOCK** (8)

Step 3: go to the bar and let your team-mates worry about it.

Multi-Choice Questions

Question: How long did the Hundred Years War actually last? Was it 100 years, 116 years or 150 years?

The occasional quizzer might think this would be a fairly tough question without the clue, but it is in fact pretty well known in quiz circles that the answer is 116 years (it ran from 1337 to 1453). So by providing choices, the quizmaster has in this case given away the answer – the 'actually' in the question clearly suggests that the answer isn't 100 years, and if it lasted 150 years why would they have called it the Hundred Years War!? Although this is a rather extreme example, multi-choice questions are often poorly constructed and can therefore be deduced quite easily with a little analysis. Of course, some multi-choice questions are just plain impossible, as in: 'How many times a year do humans blink? Is it three to five million, six to eight million or nine to eleven million?' For this type of question I can offer no advice other than when in doubt, go down the middle (which in this case would be correct) – it's just a lottery, and a rather tedious one at that.

Names

Question: Which character was played by Leslie Grantham in *EastEnders*?

If a team guesses 'Dirty Den', will that do because that is the character's accepted nickname? And indeed, would just 'Den' suffice on the basis that the more famous soap characters are often referred to by just their first names? If the quizmaster doesn't state precisely what is required, you should err on the fulsome side with your answer, in this case by writing '(Dirty) Dennis Watts', so that all bases are covered.

If you're struggling, concentrate on trying to get the surname because many quizmasters will award a half-point for that (though rarely for the first name). If you've really no idea at all, adopt the last refuge of a scoundrel and just write down 'Smith'!

Kings and Queens

Quizmaster: And now the answers to the History round. Question 1 – the father of Alexander the Great was Philip of Macedonia.

Player: Excuse me. A point of clarification, please. We put 'Philip II of Macedonia', because there was more than one of them, you know.

Quizmaster (warily): The name is fine, I don't need the number. Moving swiftly on to Question 2 – the last English King to have led his troops into battle was George II, at the Battle of Dettingen in case anyone was wondering. Which I am sure you were.

Player: Another point of order if I may.

Quizmaster (trying to ward off feeling of impending doom): What is it this time, Norman?

Player: By the logic of the previous answer, would you score a point for just putting 'George' or 'George I', or 'George CLXVIII' for that matter?

Quizmaster: What did you put?

Norman: George II, of course.

Quizmaster: So why are you asking me about hypothetical answers?

Norman: I'm just trying to be helpful, by clarifying points that may affect other teams.

Now, it is a well-known fact that your average Norman is likely to be a fully paid-up member of the Awkward Squad, so 'I'm just trying to be helpful' is but a flimsy pretext for seeking to publicly embarrass the quizmaster. But in this instance, the quizmaster has brought the problem upon himself by failing to state up front precisely what is required. With royalty, as with names, quizzers are best advised to provide the fullest answer they can.

Geeky Questions
Question 1: What is a novice in the Jedi order called? Answer: a Padawan.

Question 2: In *Star Trek V: The Final Frontier*, what was the relationship between Spock and Sybok, the film's villain? Answer: Half-brother.

Questions about certain types of science fiction programme or film defy all the usual rules of pub quizzing in that they regularly descend to depths which go way beyond normal trivia and which average quizzers find bewildering. The only answer is to delegate one of your team to immerse themselves in this stuff, or to invite a Geek or Trekkie to join you (but don't forget to bring the room spray).

Harry Potter

Question: Name any four of Ron Weasley's siblings.

'Only four? How generous!' you might observe ironically. In fact there are six, namely Bill, Charlie, Percy, Fred, George and Ginny (which, incidentally, sounds like registration time at any primary school in Muswell Hill).

The Harry Potter phenomenon has certainly transformed the pub quiz scene over the last decade. I've known players to turn puce and physically gag if a quiz does not include at least five Harry Potter questions. Am I alone in wondering why otherwise excellent quizmasters stuff their quizzes full of Potter trivia ('And, of course, the answer to Question 5 is that the emblem of the House of Skiddybriefs consists of a pair of Y-fronts flanked by two sticks of rhubarb.')

As with Geeks and Trekkies, the only way to cover yourself is for one of your team to put in the hard yards, or persuade a Harry Potter expert to join you (though it's probably best to avoid starting up too many conversations).

Top 10 Books & Plays
Pub Quiz Style!

1. Don Quizote
2. The Diary of a Nobody
3. Les Quizérables
4. A Comedy of Errors
5. Martin Quizzlewit
6. The Round of the Baskervilles
7. A Quizmas Carol
8. Bonfire of the Inanities
9. The Quiz Story of Edwin Drood
10. Geek House

Ambiguous Questions
Question: Where is Liechtenstein?

Well, for a start, it's in Europe, and it is also Alpine. More specifically it sits between Switzerland and Austria, but which answer does the quizmaster actually want?

In order to avoid trying to second-guess the quizmaster, it is perfectly reasonable to ask him precisely what he's looking for. If he's not prepared to provide clarification, your best bet is to cover all bases by writing something like: 'In the Alps between Switzerland and Austria'. And then to find a better quiz.

Here is another question which has more than one answer: With which sport do you associate Mervyn King?

Answer: Darts (BDO finalist 2002 and 2004). Oh, and bowls (World Indoor Singles Champion 2006). Bugger! There are two of them! And if running the Bank of England was a sport (and some might say ...), then there'd be three possible answers!

Ditto with Roger Taylor – there are two drumming Roger Taylors, one with Queen and the other with Duran Duran.

Questions with out-of-date answers
Question: What is the longest suspension bridge in the world?
The best approach here is to simply write 'The Humber Bridge' and you will probably earn the point, even though your answer will be incorrect. The Humber Bridge was indeed the longest such bridge when it was completed in 1981, and remained so until 1998, but it has since been overhauled by a number of others, and there's every chance that no one in the pub will have heard of any of them – I certainly hadn't when I last checked. You'll get your point because the clumsy quizmaster will have taken the question from an out-of-date quizbook and not thought to have validated it against a current on-line source such as Wikipedia.

Years Either Side

Question: When was the Domesday Book completed? I'll give you ten years either side.

The ten-year tolerance should help you home even if your team is not entirely sure of the answer. Some people might guess 1066 (on the basis that people called Norman love keeping records and will have wasted no time after Hastings in completing their documentation), while others will simply know that the exact answer is 1086. But either way, a quick discussion will confirm that 1076 will guarantee full marks.

DITLOIDs

The word DITLOID stands for (One) Day In The Life Of Ivan Denisovich, a cheery little novel by dissident Russian writer Aleksandr Solzhenitsyn. This itself is a DITLOID, which is represented by 1 = DITLOID, and the purpose of the question is for teams to identify a saying (or in this case a book title) from the combination of a number plus an acronym. Other examples of DITLOIDS include:

3 = TAL ('Three Times a Lady')

70 = SLOAM (Speed limit on a motorway)

92 = ANOU (Atomic number of Uranium)

With DITLOIDs it's best to focus initially on the number because it's the more simple component and can point you immediately in the right direction – after all, how many things can be associated with the number 92? Also, you should become familiar with some of the most common families of DITLOIDs such as atomic numbers, 'The Twelve Days of Christmas' or the number of players in sports teams, whereupon the acronyms themselves will start to offer useful clues.

That said, once the twilight army of DITLOID creators really hits its stride, things can get very challenging, for example:

🍺 54 = C in a D with the J (cards in a deck with the jokers)

🍺 64 = YOWIHYSNM (years old when I hope you'll still need me)

🍺 176 = VITLP(ITHB) (verses in the longest psalm (in the Holy Bible))

Even here, however, it's surprising how quickly one can become familiar with the rhythm of the DITLOID, lists of which can be downloaded from particularly tragic websites, so just keep reading and practising and you may be pleasantly surprised.

Arithmetical Conundrums

🍺 **Question:** A man has 132 sweets. He gives three elevenths to his eldest son, who gives one third of these to his cousin. The man then gives half to his second son, who in turn gives 17 to his uncle etc., etc.

Long-winded questions like this are irksome. They take an age for the quizmaster to read out and usually have to be repeated several times, inciting the more irascible quizzers to come up with a few of their own, such as: 'If a quizmaster asks an arithmetical conundrum which annoys me so much that I feel compelled to stab him in the eye with my pencil and then punch him in the face, what are the chances of him never doing it again? (I'm prepared to allow you 5 per cent either side.)'

The simplest way to approach questions like this is to delegate one person to worry about them, rather than having the whole team distracted – most teams will have someone with an aptitude for this type of puzzle. If not, draw lots, or simply write the question off as a *nul points* jobbie and focus on the handout sheets instead, where there will be more marks to be gained.

'True Or False' Questions

🍺 **Question:** In Alaska it is illegal to whisper in the ear of someone who is moose-hunting – true or false?

The answer happens to be 'True', but most players' reaction to this will be that the quizmaster must be confusing them with someone who gives a damn. Two iron laws of True or False questions:

1. They are always rubbish; and

2. My team always gets them wrong.

From bitter experience, the best approach I can offer is that teams should debate the question carefully and logically in order to arrive at a measured conclusion – and then write down the complete opposite!

If you are really unlucky you might have to endure an entire True or False round. One approach here is to write down 'True' against each answer on the basis that, by the law of averages, you should get 50 per cent (and you may indeed score 100 per cent where the questions have been set by a particularly sadistic quizmaster).

Talking of entire rounds, that is where we are off to next, because the one thing worse than a tricky question is ten of the buggers!

TIPS FOR TRICKY ROUNDS

The more traditional quizzes comprise ten themed rounds based on the 'classic' categories such as History, Literature, Science, Nature, Food and Drink etc., and we learned in the last chapter how to identify the type of knowledge needed to deal with these. However, a variety of more specialised rounds can often occur in pub quizzes these days, and some of them may be troublesome. This section examines a number of these more tricky rounds and provides a range of hints and tips for coping with them.

The Audio Music Round
Most Music rounds take the form of playing clips from tracks, and asking teams to write down the artist and maybe the title of the song. Until relatively recently, quiz teams could get by with a broad knowledge of 1960s and 70s pop, because at that time most quizmasters' idea of variety was to include the odd one-hit wonder such as Whistling Jack Smith ('I Was Kaiser Bill's Batman'), Keith West ('Excerpt from a Teenage Opera') or Napoleon XIV ('They're

Coming to Take Me Away, Ha Haaa!'). Those were the days, eh? Er, no, actually. But as the decades have passed and younger quizmasters have come through, a far greater blend of musical genres now features in pub quizzes, and an increasingly common approach is to include a spread of tracks from the last 50 years. In fact, this can extend right up to the present day, so teams will need to know their Tinchy Tempah, er, Tiny Cruz, er, Plan D (sorry, I'll have to come back to you on those). Perhaps the last straw for my team was when we guessed 'Bush' to the question: 'What does the "B" in Katy B stand for?' In short, teams now need a range of music knowledge, including a little classical and songs from the shows. Therefore, the simplest way for the traditional type of pub quiz team to score well on music is to bribe some younger folk to join them, in order to provide a little balance.

But if that isn't possible, here are some specific tips:

1. Get to know your quizmaster's tastes – they just can't resist inflicting them upon their captive audience in all their naffness.

2. Listen out for the title in the clip – it's surprising how often these are inadvertently included by careless quizmasters!

3. Where the clip stops immediately before the chorus, focus on the most enthusiastic teams (the ones where the hairy guys are air-guitaring along to the tracks) in case they mouth or even sing the title as the music goes quiet.

Picture Rounds
The classic Picture round contains ten or twelve photos of a selection of famous people from different walks of life – maybe a pop singer, a historical figure, a golfer, a politician, a soap star, a dead actor, someone who's been in the news that week, etc. Here are a few tips for spotting them:

■ Ask for a second copy of the sheet, so that players on both sides of the table can see the pictures. This will save half the team from having to peer through the back of the sheet, trying to identify faces from ghostly outlines that turn out to be their team-mates' thumbs.

■ If you have some idea about one of the pictures but aren't entirely sure, write down your suggestion underneath the picture (in pencil) and put a question mark after it as a clear indication that it needs verifying.

■ Ensure that everyone checks each suggestion – it's amazing how often people don't read what someone else has put and merely assume that it must be correct.

■ Place your hand over the subject's hair or headgear. This will give a specific view of the face, which may trigger something, particularly if they've been photographed in some kind of disguise.

■ Check back over your answers to the main quiz – some of the more cunning quizmasters like to include people in the Picture round who have been the subject of an earlier question.

Of course, the pictures do not have to be of people, and this can often make things even tougher. For example, my team was winning one quiz until the very last round, which turned out to be a sheet of pictures of different breeds of dog. Now don't get me wrong, I love dogs as much as the next person (apart from those that bark, defecate or shag your leg – the dog, that is, not the next person). Unfortunately, as my whole team was of a similar mind, we found ourselves overhauled at the death by a team which included an elderly lady with a pink rinse and her bull-necked son with the words 'love' and 'hate' tattooed on his knuckles, who between them appeared to cover the whole canine gamut from Chihuahua to Staffy.

Perhaps the best approach in such circumstances is to play the percentage game, like one team who, when confronted with pictures of five types of butterfly, wrote 'Red Admiral' under each picture to garner a hard-earned point!

Dingbats

Dingbat rounds contain ten or so literal depictions of well-known sayings, a kind of static version of that 90s TV staple *Catchphrase* (or 'Catchfree-ers' as pronounced by host Roy 'It's guud but it's not raayeet' Walker). For example, NOONT = Afternoon Tea, while, more cryptically, IJKLMN signifies Water (the letters link H to O – duhh!). Some players simply gobble up these visual puns whereas most of us tend to struggle. The best way to tackle these as a team is for everyone to keep coming up with suggestions (or, to use Roy's expression, 'Say what you see'), however ostensibly ludicrous, in case one of them inspires a team-mate to get the answer.

Word searches

This is where words are concealed within a grid of letters, and the key to solving them is to be systematic. The classic approach is as follows:

Step 1: Start from the top left and work across and then down, examining each square for the start of words running from left to right or from top to bottom.

Step 2: Start from the bottom right and work across and then up, examining each square for the start of words running from right to left or from bottom to top.

Step 3: Now tackle the diagonals, in similar fashion.

As with anagrams, I prefer an alternative approach which, a few seconds into Step 1, involves pretending that you've received an urgent call from someone at home that requires 15 minutes of your immediate attention.

Multiple handouts

Some quizmasters like to keep teams on their toes by peppering them with handouts and not allowing much time to complete them. The best approach when this happens is to divvy up the sheets according to individual strengths, but this can still be highly stressful, particularly for smaller teams.

Multiple handouts can also be bad news for the pub landlord because no one has time to raise their glass to their lips, let alone get to the bar for a refill. This level of intensity can stir bleak and half-remembered images of serried ranks of desks presided over by a grim-faced invigilator coldly clutching a stopwatch. As a yardstick, if the quizmaster is heard to shout: 'PUT YOUR PENS DOWN NOW', you know the handout round has got out of hand.

Memorising objects

This round is known as Kim's Game and is named after Kipling's eponymous hero, who practised this routine as part of his training to be a spy. It involves a tray of objects being displayed for one minute, after which they are covered up again, whereupon players have to write down as many of them as they can remember. The classic technique here is to study each object in turn, adding it to a story that is forming in your mind. At each stage you should create an image of the object and its role in your story, which should cement it into your short-term memory. When it comes to writing down the names of the objects, simply recount the story in your head, and the objects should present themselves to you one by one. So your story might go like this:

'I was late for work because my *alarm clock* had failed to go off. I was rushing towards the door when I noticed in the *mirror* that I had *toothpaste* on my face and my hair needed *comb*ing. And also that I was missing a *cufflink*, which turned out to be next to a *pencil* in the *ashtray.*' You get the idea, I'm sure.

Once again, while I'm not questioning the effectiveness of this technique for others, it just doesn't seem to work for me. I usually end up with something like: 'Hello, alarm clock. Is that a mirror and some toothpaste that needs combing? And did the cufflink put a pencil in your ashtray?' which I just can't seem to recall when it comes to listing out the objects.

Wipe-out

In a Wipe-out round, a team is not required to attempt every question and may leave any answer blank. Thus far, it is as per any other round. However, in the Wipe-out round, if they attempt an answer which turns out to be incorrect, they lose their entire score for that round.

This is a critical round that invariably separates the top teams when the final scores are added up. The trick is to avoid the two extremes, one of being too gung ho and the other of becoming paralysed by caution such that even the most simple answer is spurned for fear that the memory is playing tricks or the quizmaster has thrown in a 'gotcha'. As a general rule, if, following discussion, at least one player is over 80 per cent sure of the answer and no one has any strong alternative, then go for it. Otherwise you will end up agonising over whether to protect two or maybe three points while your arch-rivals are busy racking up seven or eight.

Family Fortunes

This round consists of ten or so questions where teams have to guess the results of surveys in which people have been asked an open-ended question. For example: 'We asked one hundred people to name something that drivers do with their hands when they should be on the steering wheel', to which the answers given in order of popularity were: 1 – using a mobile phone, 2 – picking their nose, 3 – smoking, 4 – fiddling with the CD player/radio.

This is a classic 'trust your first instinct' round (because, after all, that is exactly how the people polled would have approached things). One quite effective approach is for each player to write down their answer without collaborating with team-mates, and then go with a simple majority, thus not diluting people's first instincts with any discussion.

Although Family Fortunes rounds do not appeal to the more serious (i.e. po-faced) quizzers among us, they can generate a few laughs, as per these efforts from the original TV series[4]:

- Another TV game show with the word 'family' in the title: '*The Generation Game*'

- Something you open other than a door: 'Your bowels'

- A bird with a long neck: 'Naomi Campbell'

Who am I?

Another high-risk venture is the 'Who am I' round whereby teams are asked to guess the identity of a famous person from a series of progressively easier clues provided by the quizmaster as the round ticks down. A correct guess following the first clue will score ten points, then nine points following the second clue and so on. Of course, answers must be written down and handed to the quizmaster rather than shouted out, so that teams who have yet to identify the answer remain in the dark. As with the Wipe-out round, an incorrect guess will result in a zero score for the entire round.

The 'Who am I' round can be exciting, particularly if it is the final round and the scores going into that round have been read out. The leading teams will then know what they need to score relative to their main competitors to win the quiz, and will therefore need to keep a careful watch on each other's movements to help them determine when to make their guess, leading to some high-risk and potentially suicidal decision-making.

The trick here is to keep a cool head. Teams will have about 30 seconds between each question during which to decide whether to take a punt and the captain should use that time to quickly poll everyone in the team for a view. Once there are one or more people firmly in favour of a particular answer and none against, they should go for it!

Playing your Joker
The purpose of Joker rounds is to introduce a whiff of gambling into proceedings, by allowing teams to nominate a round in which to elect to 'play their Joker', thereby scoring double points for that round. Joker rounds work best when each round has broadly the same degree of difficulty, but even then you should carefully consider the breadth of a subject before committing – the broader the subject, the more dangerous it becomes to play your Joker. Taking Sport as an example, teams may be lulled into thinking this subject will be a doddle because they know their football, cricket and rugby, but then this happens:

Question 1: In which sport is the Westchester Cup contested? (Answer = Polo)

Question 2: How many players in a men's shinty team? (Answer = 12)

Question 3: What sport was originally called mintonette? (Answer = Volleyball)

Question 4: Who won Gold for Great Britain in the 1984 and 1988 Summer Olympics in the Small Bore Rifle Shooting event (Answer = Malcolm Cooper)

Question 5: At which racecourse are the Eclipse Stakes run? (Answer = Sandown Park)

Question 6: In which year was the Tour de France first held? (Answer = 1903)

10 KEY FACTS
TABLE TENNIS

1. Original nickname – wiff waff
2. Table size in feet – 9 by 5 by 2.5 high; net is 6 inches high
3. Ball – 40mm (4cm) in diameter, made of celluloid
4. Ball previously 38mm – made larger for TV, following the 2000 Olympics
5. Game won by first player to reach 11 points (previously 21)
6. Serve alternates every two points
7. Players may not wear white shirts if ball is white
8. World men's/women's team trophies – Swaythling/Corbillon Cups
9. Fred Perry – men's world champion, 1929
10. Ann Jones – ladies' world runner-up, 1957.

Subjects like Film, TV and Music are also potentially difficult candidates for the Joker Round because they are vast but also rapidly expanding, with layers of new knowledge being added on a weekly basis. Let's illustrate this by using Music as a case in point. Imagine you have played your Joker on the Music Round and the questions are as follows:

1. Which artist was No. 1 in the first ever UK singles chart published in November 1952?

2. What was the Rolling Stones' last ever No. 1 single?

3. Which 1973 hit concerned the journey of a Vietnam veteran to Spain?

4. Jive Bunny and the Mastermixers enjoyed three No. 1 hits in 1989. Name any two of them.

5. Between 1996 and 2000 nine of the first ten Spice Girls' singles reached No. 1. Name the odd one out.

6. Who reached No. 1 in 2006 with 'Put Your Hands Up For Detroit?'

7. Who featured on Olly Murs' 2011 No. 1 hit, 'Heart Skips A Beat'?

8. Novelist George Sand became the lover of which classical composer?

9. Which musical featured 'Till There Was You', which was later covered by the Beatles?

10. Which US bandleader was known as 'The Sentimental Gentleman of Swing'?

Now, you may say I have exaggerated to prove a point, but six of the seven decade-spanning pop questions relate to No. 1 singles, and the three questions at the end feature musicians that most people will have heard of. Yet I imagine many teams would struggle to get more than five out of ten, which is a lousy score on a Joker round (the answers by the way were 1 – Al Martino, 2 – 'Honky Tonk Women' (in 1969), 3 – 'Daniel' by Elton John (reached No. 4 in January 1973), 4 – 'Swing The Mood', 'That's What I Like' and 'Let's Party' (shame on you!), 5 – 'Stop' (reached No. 2), 6 – Fedde Le Grand, 7 – Rizzle Kicks, 8 – Frederic Chopin, 9 – *The Music Man*, and 10 – Tommy Dorsey).

Therefore, provided you have the relevant expertise, it's probably safer to play your Joker on more static subjects like History, Geography or Science. But if the rounds on offer are narrower in scope, for example Birds, US Geography, Mythology etc., you might be best advised to choose the most specialist subject on which to play your Joker, even though at first sight it may look somewhat scary. For example, if there is a Famous Belgians round, your immediate reaction might be to think: 'I only know about ten of them, so I'll give that a miss.' Well, chances are that so does the quizmaster, and they are the same ten, leading to a cheaply earned double-point full house for your team.

FAVOURITE PUB QUIZ CELEBRITY TEAM MATES

Respondents to a 2008 survey by digital TV channel Dave were questioned on the celebrities they consider the ideal candidates for a pub quiz team. Stephen Fry emerged as favourite (with 44.4%), followed by Carol Vorderman (38.3%), Sir Trevor McDonald (31.8%), and then chat show hosts Michael Parkinson (27%) and Jonathan Ross (22%) respectively. Least popular were David and Victoria Beckham (4.8% and 2.7%), Kate Moss (3.4%) and Jordan (5.9%).

Overall, celebrities were not seen as being the best type of team mate – only 12.5% of respondents thought that they could cut it, putting them near the bottom alongside builders (14.4%) and mechanics (11.3%). At the other end of the scale, teachers (62%) were the most popular choice, followed by journalists (53%) and cab drivers (35%).

FAVOURITE PUB QUIZ SUBJECTS

The same 2008 survey by digital TV channel Dave found that 70% of respondents claimed 'entertainment' to be their strongest pub quiz subject, followed by 'history' (28%) and 'geography' (27%).

'Sport' and 'politics' were deemed the weakest subjects with 20% and 13% respectively.

NOW TEST YOURSELF

HARD

1. Which seaside town is linked to London by the A23?

2. Which cabinet minister in the Blair and Brown governments is reputed to be a member of Opus Dei?

3. Which instrument did Glenn Miller play?

4. What was the name of Elliot's sister in *E.T.*, played by Drew Barrymore?

5. What is the connection between the above answers?

(Answers on page 127)

That concludes our journey around some of the more challenging questions and rounds that quizmasters like to chuck in to confound the unsuspecting quizzer. Time now for one final quiz fact drill; this time I think I'll go for twenty-first century gas extraction techniques – can't wait to get fracking.

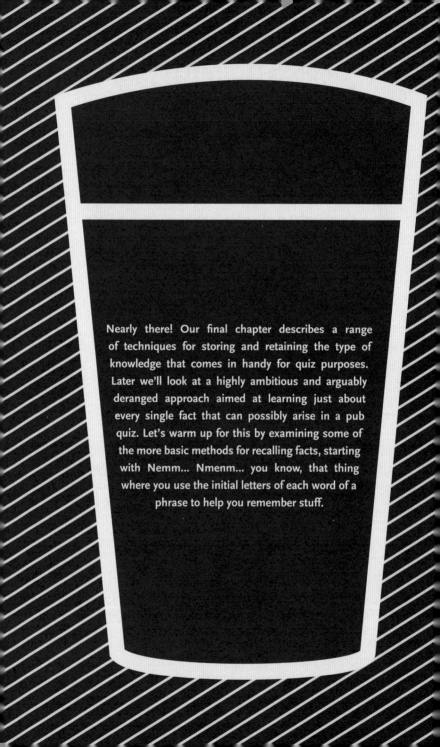

Nearly there! Our final chapter describes a range of techniques for storing and retaining the type of knowledge that comes in handy for quiz purposes. Later we'll look at a highly ambitious and arguably deranged approach aimed at learning just about every single fact that can possibly arise in a pub quiz. Let's warm up for this by examining some of the more basic methods for recalling facts, starting with Nemm... Nmenm... you know, that thing where you use the initial letters of each word of a phrase to help you remember stuff.

BLOOD, SWEAT AND BEERS

TECHNIQUES FOR LEARNING YOUR FACTS

BASIC LEARNING TECHNIQUES

Mnemonics

Not all people are familiar with the term 'mnemonic' and fewer can pronounce it without drooling. However, some of the most common ones are pretty well known – for example, 'Richard Of York Gave Battle In Vain', the initial letters of which correspond with the sequence of the colours of the rainbow (Red, Orange, Yellow, Green, Blue, Indigo, Violet). Here are some other old chestnuts:

Kent Play Cricket On Fridays, Girls Spectate

No doubt coined at some bucolic public school over a cucumber sandwich in an era when more than 18 spectators of either gender actually attended county cricket matches, this mnemonic indicates the classification system for living organisms – Kingdom, Phylum, Class, Order, Family, Genus and Species.

Men Very Easily Make Jugs Serve Useful Nocturnal Purposes

What better way can there be to remember the sequence of planets, going away from the Sun (Mercury, Venus, Earth, Mars, Jupiter, Saturn, Uranus, Neptune and Pluto)? Moreover, 'All' can be inserted before 'Jugs' if you want to include the Asteroid Belt that sits between Mars and Jupiter. And note that 'Men' and 'Mercury' start with 'Me', while 'Make' and 'Mars' begin with 'Ma' – do you see what they've done there?

But why stop there? Why not make up your own? Here are some of mine:

Perhaps You'd Get On Better Respecting Greeks

They say that every cloud has a silver lining, and perhaps the main consolation for the Greek people to have emerged from their financial crisis is that it has spawned this mnemonic for remembering the official colours of the Euro notes – Purple (500), Yellow (200), Green (100), Orange (50), Blue (20), Red (10) and Grey (5).

High Heels Leave Beryl Bored, Can Not Offer Fun Nights

The initial letters of this admittedly bizarre sentence correspond with those of the chemical elements with atomic numbers one to ten (Hydrogen, Helium, Lithium, Beryllium, Boron, Carbon, Nitrogen, Oxygen, Fluorine and Neon). It's undeniably clumsy but there are hooks like 'Beryl' (for Berylium) and 'Bored' (for Boron), not to mention the 'Hi' and 'He' word beginnings to help distinguish hydrogen from helium (or I suppose you could also say 'heels' in a high voice to mimic the effect of swallowing helium, but make sure you warn your team first).

Kennedy Would Ravish (Feverishly) Jackie's Legs

Borderline kinky, I know, but an unforgettable phrase to help recall the names of the Presidents on each US coin (Kennedy 50 cents, Washington 25, Roosevelt (Franklyn D) 10, Jefferson 5 and Lincoln 1).

All Pretentious Artists Take Great Care Lest Vicious Liars Serve Scornful Criticism

This rather extravagant mnemonic depicts the sequence of the star signs across the calendar year, starting with Aquarius, and it really trips off the tongue, doesn't it? But it works for me, though I do find that I need several minutes plus a whole side of A4 if the question asked is something like: 'October 29th falls under which star sign?'

Status Quo's Chords Make Songs Boring

If (like so many others) you struggle with the sequence of the lengths of musical notes, help is at hand in the form of this mnemonic which equates to Semi-quaver, Quaver, Crotchet, Minim, Semibreve and Breve. I do feel somewhat guilty about piggybacking on the lazy cliché that the band only play three chords – in fact I've been a fan right since the early days when you could get in to see them for about a pound (a case of *Quid pro Quo?*). But here again, once learned, never forgotten.

Might Just Reach Me Some Booze Now Mate

No more large wine-bottle-size forgetfulness misery, because we can now remember their progression – Magnum (2 x standard bottle), Jeroboam (4x), Rehoboam (6x), Methuselah (8x), Salmanazar (12x), Balthazar (16x), Nebuchadnezzar (20x) and Melchior (24x).

God Evades Letting Noah Drown

Maintaining the biblical theme, this one relates to the first five books of the Old Testament (or Pentateuch), namely Genesis, Exodus, Leviticus, Numbers and Deuteronomy.

Really Wacky Bunch

Do you ever struggle to remember the colours of the flag of those crazy Dutch people? Well, they are, from top to bottom: Red, White and Blue (with not a trace of orange in sight, surprisingly). And from the Netherlands in 1830 emerged the nation of the mighty Belgians, those Bally Young Rascals, whose flag, from left to right, is Black, Yellow and Red.

Heavyweight Men Would Like Fat Biddies For Sex

Saving the best till last, what simpler way could there be to recall the eight traditional boxing weight classes – Heavy, Middle, Welter, Light, Feather, Bantam, Fly and Straw? This is political incorrectness gone mad.

So what's the key to a good mnemonic? Two keys actually – the phrase must be memorable, and it should also be relevant to the topic concerned, otherwise you might remember that you have a mnemonic for a particular fact, but then fail to recall what it actually is (believe me, I've been there). Not all the ones shown above pass both tests but, over a period of time, they simply become engrained.

Some More Basic Learning Techniques

Techniques such as word association can also be useful when trying to differentiate related facts. For example, back in the day, most schoolboys learned to distinguish stalactites (which grow from the ceiling) from stalagmites (which grow from the floor) by thinking of mites going up and tites coming down. And it's quite easy to coin some of these yourself, for example:

Monkeys and Ponies

Following *Minder*, Delboy, *EastEnders* and all the subsequent geezer movies, most people will have come across the terms 'monkey' and 'pony' as part of the traditional argot of the Cockanese tribe. Indeed, some may also know that one is worth £25 and the other £500, but which is which? In fact this is easily remembered with the aid of a little alliteration, because the monkey is mighty whereas the pony is puny (sweet, innit?).

US golfers and UK telephone numbers

Just occasionally, a numerical sequence happens to neatly coincide with an alphabetical one. For example, following a series of mainly non-US winners, the British Open Golf Championship became dominated for a spell in the mid to late 1990s by American players – John Daly (1995), Tom Lehman (1996), Justin Leonard (1997) and Mark O'Meara (1998), which is fortunate because their surnames run alphabetically. In similar vein, the nightmare of trying to memorise some of the main UK dialling trunk codes is alleviated by the alphabetical sequence: 0121 (Birmingham) 0131 (Edinburgh), 0141 (Glasgow), 0151 (Liverpool), 0161 (Manchester), 0171 and 0181 (No longer used) and 0191 (Tyne and Wear). Don't mock – that's what it takes.

Blood pressure in Central Africa

The two blood-pressure readings are diastolic and systolic, but which is high and which is low? Try saying 'diastolic' in a low voice, followed by 'systolic' in a higher voice and repeat several times like a mantra. I also use this technique (with slightly less vocal fluctuation) to remember Kigali and Bujumbura, which are the capitals of those two pesky Central/East African neighbours Rwanda and Burundi (the initial Bs being the key to remembering which capital belongs to which country).

Who ate all the πs?

For those among us whose lives are incomplete unless we can recall the exact value of π (pi) to 8 decimal places (3.14159266), there is always: 'may I have a small cafetiére of coffee please' (count the letters in each word).

Gemstones

In my early quizzing years, the months associated with gemstones were beyond me – too difficult and way too girly. Then, one by one, they started to fall into place, as follows:

Month	Gemstone	Order learned	How learned
January	Garnet	2	King Alf (Garnett) the 1st
February	Amethyst	4	Both are quite long words, with a prominent Y
March	Aquamarine	12	The only one left!
April	Diamond	1	My birthday, and I'm a real diamond geezer (Sweet!)
May	Emerald	9	County Mayo in the Emerald Isle
June	Pearl	10	June Whitfield – twinset and pearls
July	Ruby	3	Both *u*y
August	Peridot	11	It's peridot (very hot) in August
September	Sapphire	5=	Both begin with S
October	Opal	5=	Both begin with O
November	Topaz	7=	Two Ts at the end; second letter O in month and stone
December	Turquoise	7=	Two Ts at the end – the other one!

Bizarre and seemingly random, yet its combination of instinctive association and creative logic does the job for me – what's not to like?

Doing quizzes

Simply participating in a regular pub quiz is guaranteed to improve your level of knowledge. Experienced quizzers often categorise questions into three groupings:

1. Those they already know the answer to (which tend to be their favourite sort of questions!)

2. Those they don't know the answer to and really don't care about when they're told – good quizzes should have few, if any of these

3. Those they don't know the answer to but find interesting when they're told

Embracing the last category with enthusiasm is the key to improvement because you'll come away from any decent quiz having learned a bunch of new facts that are self-evidently valuable for future quizzes. Failure to do this can lead to that incredibly annoying feeling some weeks later when the question recurs of: 'Damn! This one came up quite recently and I know we got it wrong then but I still can't remember what the answer is.'

Attending quizzes will also immerse you in the sort of classic trivia which one rarely encounters outside of the quizzing realm. For example:

- Which company was responsible for Father Christmas's cloak becoming commonly depicted as red instead of green? (Answer: Coca-Cola, by way of their 1930s Christmas advertising campaign)

- What colour is a Polar bear's skin? (Answer: Black)

- From which country do Panama Hats originate? (Answer: Ecuador)

- What is the only word in the English Language ending in 'mt'? (Answer: 'Dreamt', plus derivatives like 'Undreamt')

- What is the only word in the English language containing three consecutive double letters? (Answer: 'Bookkeeper' plus derivatives like 'Bookkeeping')

It's useful to make a note of these as and when they arise so you can revisit them at home when stress levels are lower and commit them to memory, because they will come up again and again.

10 KEY FACTS

HARRY S. TRUMAN

1. 33rd President of USA (1945–53)
2. S stands for nothing!
3. Franklyn D. Roosevelt's vice-president for just three months (January–April 1945)
4. Attended Potsdam Conference in mid-1945, following FDR's death
5. Authorised dropping of the atomic bomb on Japan
6. Sacked General Douglas MacArthur during The Korean War
7. Launched 'Fair Deal' programme of social legislation
8. Instituted 'Truman Doctrine' to contain Communism
9. Quote: 'If you can't stand the heat, get out of the kitchen'
10. Sign on desk: 'The buck stops here'.

Watching quiz programmes

There are a ton of quiz programmes on TV, particularly during late afternoon. I won't bother to list them – they keep changing anyway as new formats are tried out. But they all involve general knowledge, which is transferable to your pub quiz, so they are well worth catching, and some are highly entertaining (like that legendary edition of *Eggheads* broadcast in 2010 which featured The John Bull's narrow and heroic defeat, despite a quite brilliant performance by one of its team in roundly beating Judith Keppel on Music). They can also throw up moments of unwitting hilarity, as witnessed by the following gems, which have been widely reported over the years:

Question: *Name a film starring Bob Hoskins that is also the name of a famous painting by Leonardo da Vinci.*
Contestant: Who Framed Roger Rabbit (Rock FM – Preston)

Question: *What is the nickname of snooker player Jimmy White?*
Contestant: Hurricane Higgins (*The Chase*)

Question: *In which film did Dudley Moore star as the title character?*
Contestant: 10 (*Weakest Link*)

Question: *What was Gandhi's first name?*
Contestant: Goosey? (*University Challenge*)

Question: *What happened in Dallas on November 22nd 1963?*
Contestant: I don't know, I wasn't watching it then (GWR FM – Bristol)

Question: *What was Bram Stoker's most famous creation?*
Contestant: Branston Pickle (Sarah Cox Show – BBC Radio 1)

And we can't let these pass without including the *University Challenge* classic:

Paxman: What is another name for cherrypickers and cheesemongers?
Contestant: Homosexuals?
Paxman: No, they are regiments in the British Army, who will be very upset with you.

Reading quizbooks

Browsing through quizbooks is a very productive way of acquiring knowledge, keeping in mind of course that they are of varying quality and inevitably become out of date (aka the Humber Bridge syndrome). Also, a quite astonishing number of quizzes are instantly available on-line, albeit with the same caveats.

In particular, this is a highly effective way to master unfamiliar subjects. As you work through, you'll be pleasantly surprised how quickly questions start to recur, because there are only so many 'quiz-friendly' facts out there, particularly in the case of more specialist topics such as Food and Drink –

remember the Sussex Pond Pudding? The upshot is that, with a concerted effort, you will quickly find that you become proficient from a quizzing perspective in subjects you might have assumed would be forever closed to you.

Another major benefit of browsing through quizbooks is that you get to enjoy more room on public transport. For example, a young woman steps aboard a busy train and sees there are only three vacant seats. She thinks: 'Shall I grab the seat next to the guy with his headphones on? No, I really hate the track he's playing – the one that goes "tchii tchii tchii". Or what about sitting next to that bloke hosting an international conference call? Errrm, nope. Ah, I know, the seat next to that middle-aged man will do. He looks a bit weird but he's got his head buried in a book so it should be fine.' Then, as she draws nearer, her expression changes to one of horror: 'Omigod!!! He's reading a quizbook!!! I can't sit there in case (a) he asks me to test him on sea areas, (b) he has terminal BO or (c) he starts telling me about his yoghurt pot collection.' And so our quizzer remains free to sprawl across two seats all the way into London.

Being generally in*quiz*itive

As a dedicated quizzer you should be alert to new facts at all times of the day (or night), whatever you're doing, be it reading, surfing the web, watching telly, walking around town, or simply chatting to family and friends. And by using the fact-filleting techniques learned in Chapter 4, you will soon become proficient at distilling this avalanche of data into a concise set of valuable pub quiz facts, thereby helping you make a significant improvement in your team's performance.

Remember to keep that pen and paper to hand – if you find you have to whip it out in mid-conversation, then so be it. Simply be prepared to shrug off the resultant scorn, because you know you're heading somewhere truly magical, where they can't follow you.

Top 10
Quiz Films

1. Factual Attraction
2. Quizmaster and Commander
3. Desperately Seeking Clues Man
4. The Round of Music
5. Harry Pot Luck and the Prisoner of Askagain
6. Grumpy Old Men
7. Geeky Friday
8. The Quizzes of Madison County
9. Close Encounters of the Nerd Kind
10. The Dork Knight Rises

That covers some of the simpler techniques for learning quiz facts. Now we're going to take things up a notch, by describing how to throw a structure around all this so that the vast array of facts you are accumulating can be stored and retrieved.

ADVANCED LEARNING TECHNIQUES

OK, let me state up front that this section comes with a health warning. We are now leaving behind the sunny uplands of the gentle hints and tips described above. Instead, we are heading into the nether regions of the quiz-obsessive (if you get my drift), to a place where the entire realm of mankind's knowledge falls within our scope. In short, this is hardcore.

The author's story
Imagine setting yourself the goal of writing down every single piece of knowledge that could ever come up in a pub quiz. For the last ten years that's basically what I've been trying to achieve, by compiling a quiz fact base

which now stretches to 20 hardback files stuffed with some 5,000 sheets of A4 pages, each packed full of quiz-related facts. Here's a condensed diary of how this all came about:

1994 (age 40): On a pre-Christmas break, I rediscover an interest in History (dormant since school), and start jotting down some notes.

Late 1990s: History now a passion. Start attending the odd pub quiz but am totally useless (apart from History questions, though I'm still getting a number of these wrong – some of the questions seem awfully trite).

Early 2000s: Stop working full-time. Decide to become Renaissance Man, studying art, Shakespeare, classical music, etc. Still rubbish at quizzes.

2003: Decide it's time for Renaissance Man to become Pub Quiz Man. Throw away extensive notes on the construction and content of Shakespeare's plays and their timeless relevance etc., and start compiling simple lists of characters, quotes and other key facts/trivia (e.g. the stage direction 'Exit pursued by a bear' occurs in *The Winter's Tale*).

2004: Apply new ruthless logic to History – get rid of wishy-washy stuff like 'Causes of First World War'; instead document hard data – monarchs, PMs, dates, trivia etc. Am suddenly able to answer the trite questions as well!

2005: Realise that complete ignorance of Film is massive weakness, so document key facts on 1,000 movies. Feeling proud, report achievement to wife who observes: 'Good thing you haven't been wasting your time up there.' Undeterred, stride boldly on, setting myself task of filleting all remaining key facts from the 50 or so quizbooks that are in my study.

2006: Apply new fact-oriented approach to stuff I'd previously thought I wasn't bad at – Sport, Music, TV and Geography. Wow! What a difference! Have progressed from being rubbish to OK at quizzes.

2007: Start to tackle the other main subjects – Food and Drink, Religion and Mythology, Science, Nature and Literature (don't actually read any books, of course – no time for such luxuries).

2008: Put together a Miscellaneous File to mop up all other bits and pieces under some 30 headings, e.g. abbreviations, gemstones, etc. Quiz prowess now improving significantly – am becoming genuine all-rounder.

2009: Database now substantially complete – all 20 files of it. Throw a celebratory party for my wife, my two sons and all of my friends – a superb evening is enjoyed by the four of us.

2010: Implement systematic approach to working through all 20 files to ensure knowledge is retained, allowing myself no more than three months to get round the whole lot before the cycle must restart. Plan weekly, sometimes daily, revision schedules to ensure this is accomplished. Notice that sons seem to want to resist any attempts by me to start a conversation these days – must be the age they've reached.

2011: Am now pretty good at quizzes, but realise that, having started so late in life, I am never going to be a true contender – just the quizzing equivalent of a good club player in tennis or golf. Retire from work altogether, but fail to use this as a springboard to push revision schedule even harder. For the first time, I start to question my whole direction with my quiz fact base – which of us is the Daddy?

2012: Go into maintenance mode (i.e. continue to keep database up to date, but stop striving to commit the entire thing to memory) and relax a little. Decide that writing about quizzes might be therapeutic, hence this book. And, of course, carry on quizzing!

And that is roughly how a spark of curiosity that ignited around the time that Boyzone enjoyed their first hit ('Love Me For A Reason' – reached No. 2 in December 1994) morphed into the monster that now dominates my study, demanding to be fed with its daily diet of updates.

Creating a quiz fact base

As with all types of database, getting the structure right is key. Here is a five-step plan for creating your very own quiz fact base:

Step 1: Organise the whole wide world of knowledge into a workable super-structure such as Geography, History, Literature, Movies, Music, Science, etc. – the classic quiz round categories

Step 2: Sub-divide each major category into manageable sections, e.g. History into UK, Europe, US, World and Ancient

Step 3: Break each section down into bite-sized chunks, e.g. UK History into Pre-1066, Middle Ages, Tudors, Stuarts, Georgian, Victorian, twentieth and twenty-first centuries

Step 4: Apply further breakdowns as needed, e.g. twentieth-century Britain into decades

Step 5: Populate the database with all your painstakingly assembled sheets of key quiz facts (see Chapter 4)

It's a toss-up as to whether it's better to maintain a quiz-fact base by hand or on the PC. Mine is largely manual apart from certain sub-sections, for example UK No. 1s, where it was easier to print something from the web in order to get the page started, for subsequent handwritten annotation and updates. The data is all physically sorted and indexed so it's easy enough to pull a file down from the shelf, find the necessary entry and read or update it as required. That said, I imagine many people undertaking something similar now would probably use a computer (assuming they're allowed one on the psychiatric ward).

Keeping it up to date

Not a single day will pass without the keen quizzer discovering five, maybe ten or even fifty facts that will need to go into the database. They may be new developments such as a celebrity match-up, or old facts you simply weren't aware of until they came up at last night's quiz. The key to keeping the database up to date is to systematically extract all these facts and document them while they are still warm.

I have already stressed the importance of keeping a pen and paper to hand, and this is where something called the Transfer Sheet comes into play. The Transfer Sheet is simply a sheet of A4 on which to jot down any facts you come across as your day unfolds, which will need to be recorded for subsequent investigation and entry into the database. Here's how a Transfer Sheet might get populated over the course of 24 hours:

8am: Catch up with the news and record any new facts onto a blank sheet of A4 – this is today's Transfer Sheet (TS). Do weekly on-line checks such as chart updates or film reviews and note anything of relevance onto the TS.

9.30am: Pop into town for errands, taking the TS (folded) in pocket. Note anything new that comes to mind, maybe the name of a different variety of potato on display in the supermarket (do you have a problem with that?). Late morning and lunchtime: Update TS with new facts learned from browsing though quizbooks.

2.00pm: Go for walk, again taking TS, this time to capture any errors when doing mental quiz fact drills (e.g. Open Golf Champions since 1980) while strolling in park (and your point is?).

Late afternoon and early evening: Update TS with new facts arising from TV quiz shows, early evening news, and even teatime conversation (unlikely, I accept).

9pm: Take TS to Pub Quiz and log any wrong answers.

11.30pm: Put TS at side of bed in the event of waking up with head buzzing with a critical question that will need logging and researching.

12.45, 2.00, 3.30, 4.30 and 5.45am: Log critical questions onto TS.

7am: Google each entry on TS, fillet out key facts and update database. Throw away yesterday's TS and start a new one.

Committing it to memory

If you don't use it you lose it, so the final challenge is to somehow find a way of retaining in your head the half a million or so facts that might by now be stored in the database. In addition to some of the basic techniques such as mnemonics that were discussed earlier, there are two more hardcore methods I'd like to highlight:

Quiz fact drills

As we've seen, this involves memorising useful lists such as:

- Best Film Oscar winners (1928 to present day)

- First Division/Premier League Champions since 1960

- US state capitals and their nicknames

- Kings and Queens since 1066

- Phonetic alphabet (Alpha, Bravo, Charlie etc.)*

- Signs of the Zodiac, wedding anniversaries, gemstones

- Collective names for animals

*By the way, referring back to the question posed in Chapter 1, Romeo is the Shakespeare character that comes between the Canadian City (Quebec) and the 1980s car (Sierra).

The great thing is that you can test yourself whenever you want, though this is probably best done when you're alone (which you may find becomes your default setting anyway).

Cycling through the fact base

Not literally, of course, though it's probably big enough to house a medium-sized velodrome. This involves ploughing through each file on a regular basis to ensure the contents don't fade away over time. As a yardstick, you should aim to go right round the fact base every three months or so. This isn't as arduous as it might seem, particularly if you grow to love your facts (I know it's sad, but I'll look at one of my pages, say real names of 70s pop stars and think: 'My, my. I remember when I first started you off back in August 2006 with only a handful of tentative entries, but just look at you now.')

A Health Warning!

As I said earlier, these advanced learning techniques are pretty hardcore and the key to maintaining this level of intensity is to stay positive, and regard each fact as a new friend waiting to be made. Otherwise the process may start to overwhelm you such that every new fact becomes a threat, rather like that *Blackadder* episode where Dr Johnson has his dictionary ready to be published only for Edmund to keep thwarting him with made-up words! Whatever else may happen, I certainly do not want to be held responsible for having caused some kind of psychological collapse in any of my readers. In fact my crack team of lawyers has instructed me to draw your attention to the following behavioural checklist to ensure that your emotional wheels do not start to fall off:

1. Stay sane

2. Keep hold of your partner (assuming you have been able to attract one)

3. Remain in touch with family and friends

4. Hold down your job

5. Get to bed before 3am

6. Wash and put on clean clothes each day

7. Leave the house occasionally

You are strongly advised to consult this list at least once a week and if you find yourself slipping against any of these benchmarks, then walk away from the quizzing self-improvement programme until you feel your life is getting back on track. When you are ready to resume, you should ease your way back in with a pared down daily regime of no more than two quiz fact drills and three quiz shows, with an upper limit of twenty new facts per day. As you regain your health and strength, step things up gradually until you get back to your normal level of knowledge acquisition and retention so that you may safely resume your journey towards quizzing immortality.

NOW TEST YOURSELF

VERY HARD

1. In which year did Harold succeed Edward the Confessor as King of England?

2. In which year did the Challenger space shuttle and the Chernobyl nuclear disasters occur?

3. In which year did both Mark Twain and King Edward VII die?

4. In which year was Mark Twain born and Princess Victoria celebrated her 16th birthday?

5. What is the connection between the above answers?

(Answers on page 127)

A CONCLUSION (OF SORTS!)

And that marks the end of our quizzing odyssey. I've tried to cover all aspects of what it takes to become a pub quiz winner, from understanding what you need to know through to the hard graft of learning it all, plus a range of advice on developing a winning mentality, the value of teamwork, exploiting the quizmaster's style and staying the right side of the cheating line. If you follow this guidance with discipline and enthusiasm, the pub quizzing world will be your lobster (Arthur Daley, c.1981).

So now it's over to you. Start memorising those mnemonics, dive into those drills and get cycling round that quiz fact base. And then watch those Normans shuffle, twitch and gaze helplessly down at their shoes as your team deposes them to assume your rightful mantle of undisputed anorak kings. And don't forget to practise that magnanimous victory acknowledgement spiel, because, as sure as night follows day, you are going to need it.

And finally, to reiterate what I said right back at the beginning of our journey, happy quizzing. NOW GO OUT THERE AND RUDDY WELL WIN!

NOW QUIZ OFF!

NOTES AND QUIZ ANSWERS

Notes

(1)   See page 6. *The Publican*'s 2008 Market Report Survey
      (http://www.morningadvertiser.co.uk/Business-Support/How-to-be-a-
      quiz-master)

(2)   See page 12. *The Publican*'s 2008 Market Report Survey (see above)
      states that 42 per cent of pubs run a quiz. Based on a figure of c.50,000
      pubs in the UK (taken from the MBD Market Research site: http://
      www.mbdltd.co.uk/Press-Release/Pubs.htm) the number of weekly
      pub quizzes is estimated to be around 21,000.

(3)   See page 46. The team names listed are a combination of names I have
      come across over the years plus a selection from various websites and
      blogs, most notably 'dpquiz for quizmasters' (http://dpquiz.co.uk/
      special-features/379-new-quiz-team-names.html). The categorisation
      is mine.

(4)   See page 100. Examples taken from http://businessballs.com.

Recommended Further Reading

In the unlikely event that this book hasn't filled you up on pub quiz knowledge,
then why not go further and read these little beauties:

1. *Quiz Setting Made Easy*, John Dawson (2004) – 50 pages of advice for
quizmasters plus 150 pages of high-standard questions.

2. *How To Make £100 A Night As A Pub Quizmaster*, 'Dr Paul' (2009) – See
also http://dpquiz.co.uk

3. *How To Become A Quizzing Genius*, Jamie Miller (2010)

4. *An A to Z of Almost Every*thing, Trevor Montague (2010) – over 1,300 pages of quiz-oriented facts.

5. *Pears Ultimate Quiz Companion* – Jim Hensman (2002) – less bulky than the above, but falling out of date.

6. *Chambers Book of Facts* (2009) – 1,000 pages of densely packed facts.

7. *Chambers Factfinder* (2008) – shorter version of the above, more quiz-fact oriented.

8. *Oxford Dictionary of Quotations* (2009) – contains over 20,000 quotations.

9. *Oxford English Reference Dictionary* (2002) – combines comprehensive dictionary with encyclopaedic entries over 1,800 pages.

Answers to Now Test Yourself questions:

Chapter 1 – Easy-peasy: 1 – Veil, 2 – Evil, 3 – Live, 4 – Vile, 5 – They are all anagrams of each other.

Chapter 2 – Easy-ish: 1 – Nelson Mandela, 2 – Cassandra, 3 – Trigger, 4 – Trotters, 5 – *Only Fools and Horses*

Chapter 3 – Medium: 1 – Harry Redknapp, 2 – Wales, 3 – Torino, 4 – Misty Blue, 5 – Clint Eastwood films (*Dirty Harry*, *The Outlaw Josey Wales*, *Gran Torino*, *Play Misty for Me*)

Chapter 4 – Tougher: 1 – Rotavator, 2 – Minim, 3 – Kayak, 4 – Radar, 5 – They are all palindromes

Chapter 5 – Hard: 1 – Brighton, 2 – Ruth Kelly, 3 – Trombone, 4 – Gertie, 5 – Bingo Lingo (59, Brighton Line; 1, Kelly's Eye; 76, Trombones; 30, Dirty Gertie)

Chapter 6 – Very Hard: 1 – 1066, 2 – 1986, 3 – 1910, 4 – 1835, 5 – They are all years in which Halley's Comet was visible from Earth

ACKNOWLEDGEMENTS

To Rose and the boys for putting up with having a bona fide 24/7 pub quiz obsessive around the house, and particularly Alex for allowing me an insight into the writing process.

To all the sources I have used, including Dr Paul and Jamie Miller for their dynamic and interesting quizzing websites, and to John Dawson for his helpful book of tips on how to run a quiz, including a substantial body of high-quality questions.

To everyone who has contributed material for the book, not least my trusty punning lieutenants Philip and Glyn (who also has the dubious distinction of getting me into pub quizzing in the first place, thereby, in his words, 'unleashing the monster that lurked within').

To all my Suffolk and London quizzing chums, especially my team mates in Pete's Cat, The Ministry of Truth and LastMinute.com.

To Simon, that most competent of quizmasters, who possesses all of the good quizmaster traits described in the book, and none of the bad ones.

And, finally, thanks must go to all the team at Portico Books, in particular Malcolm Croft and Zoë Anspach, for taking the concept and helping transform it into the finely crafted opus that you have just finished reading.

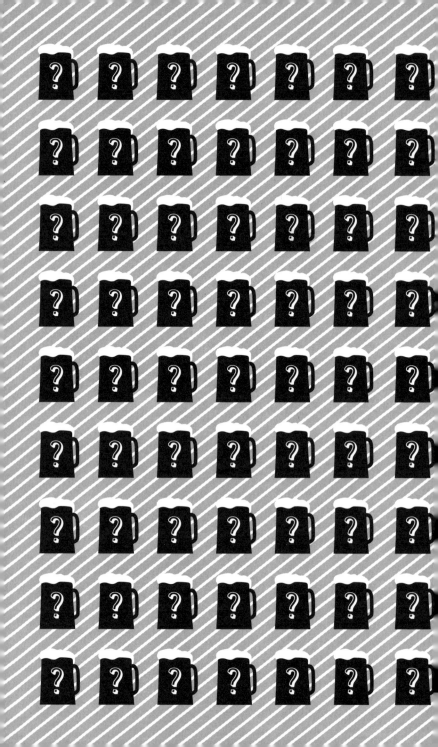